She Blew into the Room

T. E. Baker

Copyright © 2011 T. E. Baker
All rights reserved.

ISBN: 1466427183
ISBN-13: 9781466427181
Library of Congress Control Number: 2011918709
CreateSpace, North Charleston, SC

Also by T.E. Baker

A Sea Story
(A Ben Slade Novel)

Triangulation

She blew into the room like a March storm, her flimsy wet dress clinging to her every pore. All enlightened conversation at the faculty cocktail party stopped, replaced by murmurs of distain or delight, in equal proportions. Most women would have been embarrassed at being the immediate focus of attention under such circumstances. Not her. She seemed to revel in it. She made a light-hearted attempt to rearrange her wind-blown hair and approached the bartender.

Pointing to the scotch, she said in a low voice, "Give me a double, I'm late."

Ben Slade watched her from across the room. Although he tried to stop himself, he couldn't help noticing that this young lady had come to the party completely devoid of undergarments.

Retrieving her drink, she nodded to a few acquaintances and walked slowly but directly over to Ben. There was a hint of runway flounce in her gait. Few men in the room missed her progression through the clumps of guests. Certainly not Ben.

"Are you Ben Slade?" she asked. "They told me you might be here."

"Who *they?*"

Ben was a little surprised at his sharp response. He loved being around attractive women. But, somehow, there was no one more captivating than a beautiful woman who really didn't think that she was beautiful. Not so, this one. She was gorgeous and she knew it. She worked it. She was trouble.

"Sorry, Professor Slade, my name is Marie, Marie LaFontaine. I'm a graduate student in the History Department. Professor

Rawlings told me that I might find you here. 'Free drinks and all that' were his actual words." She laughed.

"George Rawlings maligns me often, and beats me at squash. Tell me, how did you know who I was?"

"George, Professor Rawlings, gave me a description. His exact words were 'he's well-preserved for someone in his mid-forties, medium height, with a short beard that still doesn't make him look like a mathematician.' Oh, and then he added—"

"That's all right. I don't need to know."

Her long auburn hair framed a classic French face with high cheek bones. No lipstick, no eye shadow. A touch of eye liner accented her light green-grey eyes which made Ben feel as if he were looking into the eyes of a wolf. A lovely wolf.

"He said that you might be willing to help me."

"What kind of help do you need? I'm a mathematician, not an historian."

"It's a fairly complicated problem, posed in a 17th century French text that I'm working on. I need someone with a mathematical mind to look at it and give me some ideas."

Ben was aware that her body language was extraordinary, but he couldn't pinpoint exactly what she was doing. She seemed to be in continuous motion. Slow, discreet, but sensual movements. His thought processes weren't helped by the fact that her cold nipples were poking at him through the fabric of her wet dress. He was starting to feel trapped. He was losing the struggle to keep his eyes and mind off the nipples.

"Well, I can't say that I don't know anything about 17th century French mathematics since we're still using most of it today. Some might say that Lagrange was the last person in the western world to have an original idea."

"Really?"

"Well, not really. If it got out, we'd all be out of a job. It's sort of a mathematicians' joke."

"I didn't realize that mathematicians had jokes," she said, suppressing her laughter.

Ben laughed, perhaps too loudly. "Of course we have jokes. A fine body of humor."

"Okay, you're on. Tell me a mathematicians' joke."

Ben paused for a moment. "All right. You've heard of Bertrand Russell, no doubt."

"Yes, of course."

"Well, he's best known for philosophy but his first interests were in mathematics. In fact he collaborated with Alfred North Whitehead to derive all of mathematics from symbolic logic. Published as *Principia Mathematica*."

"Is that funny?"

"Patience, that's just the background for the joke."

"Sorry," she said, already starting to laugh.

"So, a young Russell is meeting Whitehead for the first time in Whitehead's office. Whitehead is seated behind his desk and on his desk there's a basket of apples. Russell is a bit nervous since Whitehead is already a well-established mathematician. Russell says, 'Do you have some apples in that basket?' Whitehead frowns and says, 'No.' Russell tries again. 'Do you have any apples in that basket?' Whitehead again says, 'No.' Now Russell is getting excited. 'Do you have apples in that basket?' Whitehead jumps up and shouts, 'Yes.' The two men shake hands and are friends for life."

Ben smiled triumphantly as Marie dissolved in laughter.

"So, do you still doubt that mathematicians have good jokes?" he asked.

When Marie stopped laughing she said, "Oh, the *joke* was terrible. *You* are very funny."

He was backpedaling. Maybe his initial judgment of the girl had been too harsh. She was, after all, charming and intelligent. And her slight French accent didn't hurt.

"How did you come out in this weather without a raincoat?" he asked.

"It wasn't raining when I left. I can never tell what the weather will do here in New England. And besides, the only waterproof coat that I own has 'TheNorthFace' in white letters on the chest. Hardly chic enough for a party like this."

"Well, this isn't much of a party and it's winding down. In honor of someone in the Physics Department who's been named to the Academy of Sciences. Don't really know him."

"Free drinks and all that?"

"Right. George was right on target, as usual."

"If you look at my problem, I'll provide you with free dinner."

"That's the best offer I've had today. I'll be happy to look at your problem. And dinner would be fine, but first you have to get into some dry clothes."

Marie looked down at her clinging dress. "Oh, you're bothered by my protrusions?" she said in a voice that half the room must have heard.

Ben was too embarrassed to respond.

Ben took her to his car and drove her to her apartment—a third floor walk-up in a clean but run-down building that catered to graduate students living on assistantships. As they entered the apartment, a sleepy-eyed, dark young man arose from the couch. Marie had a private word with him in French and he picked up his backpack and left the apartment.

"Boyfriend?" asked Ben.

"Temporary flat mate," she said, "and he had something else that he should have been doing anyway. There is an open bottle of Pinot Noir on the kitchenette counter. Pour me a glass, too."

Marie went to the bedroom and peeled off her wet dress, making no attempt to hide herself from Ben's view. Oh, well, he thought, if she doesn't care, why should I? As promised by her revealing dress, her body was spectacular. She rubbed herself vigorously with a towel and pulled on jeans and a bulky sweater. Still no undergarments. She returned to the living room brushing her hair. When she finished, Ben handed her a glass of wine.

"Here's to 17th century French problems," Ben said.

"And to your free dinner. Is Spaghetti Carbonara okay with you?"

"Sounds perfect. Can I help?"

"Keep me company while I prepare."

"Hard not to, this place is quite cozy." Ben was wondering where the 'temporary flat mate' slept since the apartment consisted of two rooms, only one of which was a bedroom.

"While I cook, I'll give you some background on the problem. In 1668, the French Crown, Louis XIV, ordered a survey of the topology of the entire country. The technique they used was called triangulation, a literal translation. I'm not sure exactly how it worked, but I suppose that it had to do with establishing triangles across France to calculate distances and heights of things that couldn't be measured directly."

"Actually, I do know a little about it. Direct application of high school geometry. But why do you need to know?"

"The text I'm working with assumes that the reader knows how it was done and gives the location of something important in terms of previously established triangles or something like that. Do you know that there are still some bronze stakes in the ground in

France from this survey and people just leave them where they are? I thought that I understood it, but nothing makes sense. Give me some background, if you will. How does it work? How would they carry out the survey? How could it go wrong?" Marie put a pot of water on to boil and continued chopping bacon and onions.

"Well, some distances are easy to measure directly and accurately. Others, like across a river or up a mountain, are not. The idea is to establish a triangle of three points that are visible from one another. You can fix the size of the triangle if you know the length of one side and the size of two angles. Or if you know two sides and the interior angle although the former was probably more useful."

"I sort of figured that much out, but how accurate could it be?"

"They had things like transits or sextants that could probably do a credible job of measuring the angles. They would also need transits or sextants with an artificial horizon to measure elevations."

"Elevations?"

"Yes, the triangles are not horizontal, remember. To get distances on the earth's surface, the triangles have to be brought down to the horizon, or projected onto the plane of the earth's surface."

"*The plane?* Is the earth flat?" She laughed again.

"I was going to say flat enough for these purposes, but with care, they could actually measure the earth's curvature. If done right, the technique would effectively produce a contour map of the terrain. It could also determine accurate latitude/longitude positions of locations in France."

"What could make the process go wrong?"

"Errors can propagate through the system."

"How so?"

"Say you start with a known distance between two points, A and B. And from each point you measure the angle between the other point and the mountain, M."

"Okay."

"That gives you the first triangle, ABM, so you can calculate the distance between each point and the mountain. Then you place another point, C, part way around the mountain to form another triangle, BCM, and repeat the measurement of angles. Now, if the new point is across a river, you may have to use the calculated distance from the old point, B, to the mountain as your distance."

"What's wrong with that?"

"Any error in the first triangle calculation will show up in the second."

"How would they have dealt with this?"

"Redundancy. More triangles. More calculated estimations of the same things."

Marie was silent for a while, mulling over the possibilities. Ben watched her rapid chopping with admiration. He felt that she certainly knew her way around the kitchen.

"*Je ne sais pas*," she said with a sigh. "I feel that I am so close, but every time I try to relate the positions in the text to latitude and longitude, I get an error, the same error. It's very frustrating."

"Let me guess," said Ben. "An error in longitude."

"Yes, yes, an error in longitude."

"Of a little more than two degrees." Ben laughed.

Marie put down the knife and faced Ben squarely. Her intensity surprised him. It was obvious that this was not a trivial academic pursuit to her.

"How did you know?" she asked.

"Because the French used Paris as the prime meridian up until World War I or thereabouts. They had a hard time accepting the

English Greenwich as the starting point for longitude, even though the rest of the world had long adopted it as the standard. Any references to longitude in a 17th century French text would have been measured from Paris."

Marie stood dumbstruck as she went over Ben's revelation. Then, in a burst of girlish enthusiasm, she threw her arms around Ben's neck and gave him a forceful kiss. Her body pressed against his from head to toe. She released him from the kiss but kept her arms around his neck as she rested her head on Ben's chest.

"I thought that you weren't a historian," she said.

"I've managed to pick up a few facts, some of them useful." Her body felt supple and soft against his. He was starting to have strong feelings for this girl, in addition to the predictable lust.

She released him as quickly as she had grabbed him and ran to the phone. After dialing a number from memory she had a short, excited conversation in French. She returned to Ben with a smile, gave him another light kiss, and resumed cooking.

"Another bottle of wine," she said. "This calls for a celebration."

Ben looked through her wine cellar, a wine rack on the floor of the utility closet, and chose a bottle of Barolo which he opened and placed on the kitchen table.

"How did you come to study history here in New England?" he asked.

"Long story," she said. "First I studied cello in France. A performance major, I think you say here. Then I realized that, although the love for the cello was great, I would never be an outstanding performer. Never famous, just okay. Third chair in a reasonable orchestra or something like that."

"Unfortunately, that realization comes late to many musicians," said Ben nodding to a cello case in the corner of the living room, "but you still play?"

"Yes, practically every day. Do you do music?

"Yes, classical guitar, although I was never destined to become a professional musician. In fact I'm still a student. From time to time I take lessons here at the conservatory."

"Wonderful, we must play sometime. Then, when I left the conservatory in France I considered following my father into medicine, but there were so many…pre…"

"Prerequisites?"

"Yes, there were so many prerequisites that I hadn't studied in music school. So after much thinking, I decided to study history, my second love after music."

"So that's the history part. Why here?"

"I was doing graduate studies at the Sorbonne and got interested in a topic involving some 17th century poetry written after the Thirty Years War. It turns out that your friend, George Rawlings, is a world-renown expert on the subject."

"Amazing," said Ben, "We've been friends for a couple of years but I've never known what his specialty was."

"Well, he has many colleagues and connections at the Sorbonne and, after some discussions, he agreed to take me on as a graduate student. So here I am."

Ben raised his glass, "Welcome to the U.S. of A."

Spaghetti done and bacon cooked, Marie finished and served the Carbonara.

"Salad after," she stated as a matter of fact.

"Agreed," said Ben, "I never understood eating a salad first."

Instead of cooking the egg with the bacon, cream, and cheese, Marie added it raw on top after everything else was in the bowl.

"Wonderful Carbonara," said Ben. "Where did you grow up?"

"Bandol, a small coastal town between Marseilles and Toulon."

"I've actually been there on a backpacking trip during my college days. A lovely spot. Must have been difficult to leave."

"I can always go back," she said.

"Brothers and sisters?"

"Two sisters, one exactly like me," she said with a smile.

"Twins? You two must have stirred things up in Bandol."

"Why do you say that?"

"Well, you by yourself caused something of a stir at the cocktail party."

"Me? How so?"

"Let's say that your entrance was a bit dramatic."

Marie laughed. "Oh, well, that was just New England greeting Provence. Yes, my father said that Bandol relaxed a little after we left."

"So, why would that be? What did you two do?"

Marie hesitated. "We don't talk about things like that the way you people do."

"Sorry, don't mean to offend, just to pry a little."

"Okay, in the interest of prying a little, Thérèse and I were identical, but *identical*. Even our father had trouble telling us apart. We loved to have fun with the confusion and caused lots of trouble. They tried to keep us apart in school so we switched classes if convenient or for a test if one of us knew the material better. We even traded boyfriends sometimes."

"Ouch," said Ben. "And the poor guys never figured it out?"

"Nobody got hurt, as they say in your movies."

"Then I agree with your father, the town could relax with you two gone."

"Thérèse never went on to university but we've remained close. For years she did some serious modeling. I would join her when I had time off."

"And pull a switch?" asked Ben.

"Yes, we did that, but sometimes we would work together. They would use both of us for a special shot. It was a lot of fun."

"But you didn't stick with it?"

"Modeling? No, I wanted to do something with my brain."

"It's nice to be able to do both."

Marie just smiled and was quiet for a while.

"And what about you?" she asked. "Where do you come from?"

"A small town north of Boston, good place to raise kids, but not a place that I would ever move back to."

"And why the pursuit of your esoteric mathematics? The right word, esoteric?"

"Yes, the right word, but it's not so esoteric once you get used to it."

"But you knew that was what you wanted to do?" she asked.

"Not really. My father wanted me to be an engineer and sent me to engineering school. Maybe because I was interested in how things worked."

"He was that…strong?"

"Yes, strong is a good description. Maybe influential would be better. After the first semester, I knew that I would never be an engineer, but I found that I loved the mathematics so I just continued on in mathematics until I ended up in topology."

"But why topology?"

"Hard to say. It seems that the more abstract mathematics becomes, the more beautiful it becomes."

"And topology is gorgeous," she said with a laugh.

"Yes, it's gorgeous. At least I used to think so."

"What has changed for you?"

"Well, as you noted at the faculty cocktail party, I'm in my forties. Nobody should expect much of a mathematician over thirty. As a mathematician, if you haven't done something great in your twenties, it's probably not going to happen."

"But what about the greats? Like the French ones you mentioned before."

"Laplace and Lagrange? Their ground-breaking work was done in their mid-twenties."

"How about Einstein? He worked into old age at Princeton."

"Right. But he had his 'miracle year' when he was twenty-six. Published three papers that shook the world. His attempts later in life at coming up with a unified field theory were unsuccessful."

"Okay, but what about Newton? He was fighting with our poor Leibniz about the invention of calculus when he was an old man," she said with authority.

"True, but he came up with the idea during the plague years when he was in his mid-twenties. He just didn't bother to publish it until later. The mathematical spark just doesn't happen when you get older."

"So your spark is gone?" asked Marie with a smile.

"Well, I'm still sparking on some cylinders."

"Which cylinders?"

"Life cylinders. Those that deal with life."

"Ah, and what do you do for fun?"

"Play the guitar, play chess, do some martial arts, and then, there's my *Emma*."

"Your Emma?"

Ben laughed. "Yes, I have a sailboat named *Emma* down in the harbor."

Marie quietly cleared the table and served salad and a cheese plate.

"Why, in English, do they use 'topology' to describe my problem and also for your field of study?" she asked.

"Your problem is geometry applied to topography. The field of algebraic topology is very different. Like studying the properties of surfaces that look like doughnuts. You know, they're solid but there's a hole in the middle. That confuses a lot of mathematicians. Some topologists don't even talk to other mathematicians."

"Oh, so there's a pecking order among mathematicians? Is that correct, pecking order?"

"Yes, it's correct and yes, there is one, at least some of us think so."

"Wow, today I learn first they have jokes and now a pecking order. So what kinds of *real* problems do you higher pecking people work on?"

"It's true that some of us ask questions that, we suspect, will only lead to other questions that can't be answered either. When we get stuck, we leave a turd and move on to the next question."

"A turd?"

"Yes, a mathematical term. Hard to explain."

"I think that I've heard that term used in another way. Maybe even stepped on one."

"Okay, they leave something objectionable for other people to deal with."

"Example, please."

"Like Fermat's Last Theorem which was really a conjecture. He had a copy of an ancient Greek text in which a particular problem was presented. He wrote—"

"Fermat was French, no?"

"Yes, but of course."

"What problem?"

"You know the Pythagorean Theorem: For a right triangle, side a squared plus side b squared equals hypotenuse c squared? Well, replace the 2, the squared part, with n. That equation with $n=2$

has integer solutions for *a*, *b*, and *c*. For example 3, 4, and 5. The ancient Greek text conjectured that there was no integer solution for *a*, *b*, and *c* if *n* was greater than 2."

"Wow, how did they know?"

"They didn't, they were guessing. So Fermat wrote in the margin of his copy of the text, 'I have a proof of this but it is too long to fit in this margin.' And he left this turd for future generations to deal with."

"Is it true and did he have a proof?"

"It *is* true, now proven laboriously, but I'm pretty sure that he just *believed* that it was true and was leaving a turd for others to deal with, which they've been doing for hundreds of years."

"Why is the proof so difficult?"

"It's a non-existence proof. It's saying that for *n* greater than 2, no integer solution exists for any *a*, *b*, and *c*."

"I see. To prove that something doesn't exist, you have to look everywhere."

"You should have been a mathematician."

"But you didn't answer my question. That equation for *n* greater than 2 is useless anyway, even if it had solutions. What about *real* problems?"

"*Real* might be problematic in this context, but ... like the four-color problem." "The four-color map problem?" she asked.

"Right, the proposition that you can color the areas, or states, of any planar map with only four colors with no two areas with an adjacent edge having the same color."

"Can it be done always?"

"Yes, and now it's been proven," said Ben with disgust.

Marie laughed. "You look like a child taking medicine."

"Well, it was proven with the help of a computer. Sort of an exhaustive list of possibilities that the computer worked through."

"What's wrong with that?"

Ben looked at her sternly. "Not elegant. It should have been elegant."

Ben pushed his chair back from the table, hoping to change the subject and wondering if he had overstayed his welcome. Marie poured him the last of the wine and took the salad plates to the kitchen. She returned to the table behind Ben and placed her hands on his shoulders, rubbing gently.

Leaning over, she almost whispered into his ear, "You Americans are like children sometimes."

Ben started to react but she held him.

"I like it," she said, stopping his protest, "and I like you."

Ben put his hand on hers and gave it a squeeze.

"Do you like me?" she asked.

"More than I should."

Marie laughed, swung one leg over Ben's lap, and straddled him. She turned up his head and kissed him hard. His hands went up her back under her sweater. She murmured in approval.

Craziness, he thought. He didn't know why this was happening, or even how, but he was not about to get in the way. Not now. Her sweater hit the floor, followed by his shirt, minus a few buttons. He stood up with her still clinging to him and made his way to the bedroom which was only dimly lit by the kitchen lights. He dropped her on the bed and tried to take off her jeans. Too tight. She lay on her back and laughed as he tugged at the cuffs. When he was successful, she reached up and undid his pants, downed his briefs, and took a moment to inspect. Apparently satisfied with what she found, she lay back down, pulling him onto her. She was already moist and he entered. So much for foreplay, he thought. Marie arched her back and raised her arms above her head. He slid his hands up her sides, slowly over her breasts, and up her outstretched arms. He took her wrists and held her as he moved rhythmically in and out. In and out. She closed her eyes and turned her head up and to one side. She lowered her back and raised her pelvis, matching his quickening movements. After what seemed like an eternity he exploded and her body stiffened as she gave a small gasp. He released her wrists and, with one hand supporting the small of her back, rolled with her onto one side while keeping their wondrous connection. She opened her eyes and smiled.

"That was very nice," she said.

"I would have to agree," he said although he was thinking that 'fantastic' might come closer to describe what he was feeling.

"I hope you don't think that I do that with everyone I meet. I'm afraid that you will think that I'm, how do you say, easy."

"I don't think that at all. I'm just surprised that you find me, well, attractive."

"Well, obviously I do."

She gently pulled away from him. Gathering some tissues from the bedside stand she slowly and meticulously proceeded to wipe him off before turning to herself. When she finished, she playfully threw herself on top of Ben. She brought her face close to his, nose to nose, and said, "So what do we do now?"

"How about slow, passionate, love making?"

"Just what I was thinking, but first a little game."

"A game?"

"*Oui, la torture chinoise*," she said with a wicked laugh.

"I'm not sure I like the sound of that."

"Lie on your back, arms out, legs apart, like Da Vinci's perfect man on a circle."

"Okay."

"Now close your eyes and don't move. I'm going to run the tip of my tongue from one or your extremes on the circle to another, like fingers to toes, taking any path I like. If you move or flinch, I get to start all over again."

"I see."

"Ready?"

"Ready."

Marie wrapped her hair around itself and put it over her shoulder to keep it out of the way. Kneeling over Ben, she started at his right foot and worked slowly up the inside of his leg. At first he could hardly tell that she was actually making contact; her touch was so soft. Then the anticipation of the next sensitive spot started to drive him mad. When she reached the inner side of his mid-thigh, he couldn't stand it anymore. He flinched.

"Ah, ha," she cried. "Just as I thought. No will power."

"Not fair. This is hard."

"That's not all that's hard," she said with a laugh. "Lie back and we'll start again."

This time Marie started at his left hand and moved down his arm to his neck, then across his chest to his abdomen and slowly down his upper thigh. It took all of his powers of concentration to put his mind somewhere else. Her hair brushed against his erection as she moved down his leg, but he remained immobile until she reached his toe. Victory, Slade.

"Okay, now it's my turn," he said.

"Oh, no, there is no turn. The game is over."

Ben picked her up by her waist and put her down on her back.

"Just one turn. It's only fair," he said.

Marie settled into the DaVinci position and took a deep breath, "Okay, give it your best shot. I love this American English."

Ben started on her left hand and moved up her arm to the inside of her biceps.

Marie jerked and screamed, "Not fair. You know too much about the body, this body."

"I would like to know more. Lie down."

Ben started again on her left hand but avoided the biceps spot to cross her shoulder, neck, and down to her breast, not to the nipple but slowly around it. Marie wriggled but didn't move enough for a foul to be called. Ben passed over the right breast and started moving down her right arm. As he reached her wrist Marie started to relax. Then Ben reversed course, went back up her arm, down her chest, and settled on her inner thigh. Marie tensed. There he stayed, moving only slightly from time to time.

Marie exploded. "You don't play fair."

She rose up and pushed him over onto his back. She sat on him and pushed his erect penis into her.

"That's fair?" he asked.

"So sue me," Marie said as she started a rocking motion.

Ben moved his hands up her torso to her breasts. She threw her head back and said something in French which Ben couldn't understand. It didn't bother him. Somehow he felt that he understood everything he needed to.

Ben awoke to the sound of the shower. It was near midnight. He joined Marie in the shower and would have made love again if she had been willing but she was quiet and distracted. She seemed to have serious things on her mind.

As they toweled off and dressed, Marie asked, "Do you read French and are you busy tomorrow for lunch?"

"*Yes*, on one and, *no*, on two," Ben answered with a laugh. "Why?"

"Well, if you like, you can take the text home. See if you can make sense out the important parts. They all are marked. I have some things to do in the morning. Then, you can take me to lunch and return the text with your comments."

Ben had been wondering how to approach the issue of seeing her again. Marie, on the other hand, seemed to have it all worked out.

"Sounds fine. Pick you up at 12:30?"

"Give me until 1:00 to be sure."

Marie produced a Prada shopping bag containing an old leather-bound text, gave him a kiss, and ushered him out the door.

"Time for some sleep," she said quietly.

"Until tomorrow. You are wonderful."

Marie only smiled and closed the door.

On his way down to the car, Ben had a chance to assess what had just happened. The assessment took the form of his inner voice, which seemed to phrase advice the way his mother used to do when he was a teenager. *Time to think with the muscle in your head instead of the one between your legs.* Sleeping with an adult graduate student probably wasn't going to get him the boot from the university, although the powers that be would certainly take a dim view of the situation if they found out. Not to mention the age gap. *You must have twenty years on her.* Didn't seem to bother her. She knew exactly what she was doing. She was in control from the start. *You could have resisted or given in. Maybe you could have resisted.* The events of the evening flashed through his mind. Her wet dress, the dinner, the conversation, her straddling him in the chair. *No, resistance would have been futile.*

As he left the building, he heard a window opening above him. He turned to see Marie leaning out of the window, merrily blowing him kisses. Ben knew that he had fallen in with a beautiful, unpredictable character who would drive him crazy if he wasn't careful.

Ben felt the need to clear his head and, for that, there was no better place than his boat. His pride and joy, a 38-foot vintage cutter named *Emma*, had been launched the previous weekend for the summer season. He had a small, old, comfortable house off campus, but he felt most at home on his boat. He drove to the marina, waved to the security guard, and settled into the pilot's seat of the raised cabin of the cutter with a cognac and Marie's text. As he started into the text he realized that sleeping with Marie was the first time he had had sex since Christine had left the previous fall. Actually it was long before Christine had left in the fall. The soft seductive southern belle Christine. The fragile sensitive earth mother Christine. The self-absorbed aggressive social climber Christine. The ex-wife Christine.

He had met Christine while he was finishing his Ph.D. at Rice. She was working on her M.A. and Mrs. which she had planned to receive together. And Ben was easy prey. He was dazzled from the first encounter. He had been in and out of relationships throughout his time in college but none had been lasting. Doing his research and getting his doctorate were all that had really mattered. With Christine it was different. Maybe it was because she was a child of the Deep South. She hailed Atlanta as home but really came from someplace a bit farther south and culturally quite a bit farther back in time. He had never been close to a woman who truly believed that the sexes were completely different, that it was useless for one sex to try to understand the other, and that you just had to revel in the differences. She slept with him almost immediately and intimated that she had been a virgin; she had been waiting for him her whole life. He was never sure about her virginity but never questioned as it didn't really matter. He wasn't a virgin, why would he impose such a requirement on his partner? She moved into his apartment and created a homey nest for two. Ben was

Triangulation

overwhelmed. In one fell swoop all of his creature comforts, those things that he didn't pay much attention to, were taken care of. She was intelligent, sexy, good company, and very soft. Very warm and very soft. And she was always thinking about those things that he never considered. She was making wedding plans before Ben proposed. They were married right after graduation.

Christine started out as a devoted faculty wife, supporting Ben in his career choice. Ben worked incessantly teaching, doing research, and publishing while making a couple of strategic moves to the University of Kentucky as Assistant Professor and then to Northwestern as Associate Professor. Christine was proud of him. She loved the fact that it was impossible to explain to her friends back in Georgia exactly what it was that her husband did. He was a math professor who studied things that nobody really understands. Finally the tenure-track offer came from this famous university in New England and Ben jumped at the chance. They had arrived, or were going to, shortly. Fantastic.

But arriving and having arrived are two different things. The finality of their situation in New England depressed her immensely. There was no more striving, no more progressing, no more brilliant unknown future, no brass ring to grab. What they had now they would have until retirement. Ben was going to get tenure, for Christ's sake. "Do you know how many chairs of topology there are in the US?" he had asked. For Christine, it wasn't enough. She found the role of professor's wife in this small university town oppressively boring.

They tried unsuccessfully to have children. The process started simply enough.

"Would you like to have children?" Christine asked.

"Sure, you know, when the time is right?"

"Is it right now?"

"Sure…I guess we're pretty much settled. Sure."

This decision was a major turning point in their relationship. After six months of thermometers, calendars, and 'sex because we have to now,' the struggle between the sexes as in *Men are from Mars, Women are from Venus* was transformed into the war between the North and the South with the despairing comment, "I've always been told that the Yankees' sperm don't count for much." Ben's first reaction was to laugh but he realized an instant later that Christine believed this bit of 150-year-old misinformation in her inner being.

She tried unsuccessfully to develop new interests. The town had no Junior League. Really, no Junior League and nothing that remotely resembled it. Her state of mind was disintegrating fast. Then she found the *house*.

The *house* was a stone cottage some two hundred fifty years old, situated near the main part of town but in a nearly inaccessible crevice in the rocks on the edge of a stream. The location of the property dictated that it was useless for almost any other purpose and thus it had remained as it was for two centuries. The narrow road that reached the house ended two doors beyond. Originally the cottage had been on the far outskirts of town, but now it was almost central and not far from the university. Years before, someone had added a second bedroom, a bathroom, and a study in a more or less modern style. At least modern for the 50's. The house was completely rundown, a place nobody seemed to want. And yet, to Christine, it was a lost puppy that simply needed nurturing. She convinced Ben to use most of his father's inheritance to make a down payment. They moved into the almost livable, modern part and Christine started the transformation. The rest of his inheritance quickly went to bringing the old cottage up to reasonable standards. Ben was immersed in researching and publishing to secure his tenure and, truth be told, he welcomed the fact that Christine was absorbed in the renovation even though it depleted their resources. Finally, they could move from the shoddy, leaky bedroom in the modern part of the house into the bedroom in the original stone cottage.

That's when they met Ezekiel. Ben had never believed in ghosts; they weren't part of his universe. Christine was much more susceptible. They had just moved their bed into the old bedroom. After dinner, Ben went into the bedroom and, inexplicably, felt something, a presence, in the far corner of the room beside the fireplace. Christine had placed an old rocking chair there because she thought it the perfect spot to be on cold winter evenings. Evidently something else felt that it was the perfect spot as well. Ben stood in the doorway for a full two minutes, questioning his senses and wondering if he had had too much wine at dinner. Ben was sure that something was there in the corner; he just couldn't accept it logically. He said nothing about it to Christine when they went to bed that night. Christine's habitual side of the bed was closer to the corner of the room where Ben had felt the…whatever it was. In the morning he found her shivering and complaining about the cold although it had been a warm night. Ben was sure that he could detect a temperature difference between his side of the bed and hers.

The next day Christine questioned some of her friends in town and was told that the cottage was supposed to be haunted by an old fisherman, Ezekiel, who had been lost at sea some two hundred years before. No wonder the property had been so affordable. Two nights later Christine arose to go to the bathroom and evidently had a direct encounter with Ezekiel. Ben could never convince her to tell him what had happened but he was sure that it must have been traumatic. In any event, at Christine's insistence, they moved back into the leaky bedroom in the other part of the house. Christine's project was not only a failure, it was now untenable.

Probably the most important factor in the demise of their relationship was the fact that Christine hated the long New England winters with a passion. Ben had his work and didn't mind the limitations of living on a professor's salary. He didn't even mind the cold and wouldn't think to wear a coat unless she reminded him. They joked about her being a tropical flower, freezing to death in the Artic. But as Ben had noted, all jokes are half serious.

The stone cottage debacle was just the capstone of a number of unhappy years. Christine moved back to Atlanta and filed for divorce. It had been finalized four months before in January leaving Ben shaken and saddened. The situation wasn't helped by the fact that Christine quickly remarried, this time to a wealthy freshman US senator from Georgia, a Republican. But Ben's friend George, during a lull in their squash game, had quipped that her pending remarriage was actually a silver lining in that it would make the divorce settlement simpler. *Yes*, Ben had replied, *all she wants is out*. Ben missed her but he honestly felt that there was nothing that he could have done to save their marriage short of finding a different career. With Christine gone Ben had moved the bed back into the old bedroom. He couldn't explain the Ezekiel phenomenon but didn't feel threatened by it.

Ben frowned as he realized that he was thinking about Christine again. Then his face broke into a small smile as he thought that he was finally getting over her, he just needed more therapy of the variety that Marie had just provided. He returned to the text but found it tough going. 17th century French wasn't his strong suit and his powers of concentration were gone for the day. Visions of Marie made sure of that. He soon turned out the light and fell asleep where he sat.

He awoke with a jolt. The cutter's raised cabin did little to shield him from the morning sun rising off the horizon. *Smote* is the word, he thought with a grin. The sun *smote* him. The text and his half-finished cognac lay before him. He had a sore neck from sleeping in an awkward position but otherwise felt refreshed. Mental Postit notes popped into his consciousness. He had to stop by his office to give his graduate assistant a copy of the final exam for his undergraduate math class. He smiled. The exam was going to cause a minor revolt. Math exams were generally one hour long and contained four problems or less. Grading the exams was tedious since partial credit was awarded even though the final result was missing or wrong. Awarded if the grader could assess that the student actually knew what he was doing. But that was the rub. The undergraduates felt that the grading process was too subjective and often complained about their grades. Not this time. Ben had constructed a multiple-choice exam with twenty questions. Unheard of in the Math Department. It had taken him two days of hard work. Almost all of the choices seemed reasonable. Most of the common misconceptions and possible mistakes were contained as options in the choices. Undoubtedly, the majority of students would leave the exam thinking that they had aced it, only to find out later that it had been more difficult than they had thought. And they wouldn't be able to complain about subjectivity. Yes, a minor revolt. He smiled again. He thought of Marie. After the office he had to go home for a shower and a change of clothes so that he could take Marie to lunch.

Ben arrived home about eleven o'clock to find that his house had been broken into and ransacked. His desk, in particular, was in shambles and every book from every bookshelf was piled on the floor. Other than the mess, there was very little damage and it didn't look like anything was missing. Ben was more perplexed than angry. He called the police.

The small, university town had one detective, Richard Townsend, a difficult man of limited social skills who had worked his way up through the ranks. In appearance, he seemed to be modeled after Tom Landry, the coach of the Dallas Cowboys during their heyday. Tall, lean, and erect with a narrow brimmed hat, narrow tie, and a dark grey suit.

Detective Townsend, as he liked to be called, took pride in the way he handled his job and felt that he was the intellectual equal of 'any of those fancy professors in town.' The truth of the matter was that he felt frustrated that the small, New England town seldom required the kind of police work that he was capable of providing. His major efforts in the past months involved trying to thwart the annual placement of a carriage from the local museum on top of town hall by the graduating seniors. He had been unsuccessful.

Detective Townsend arrived at Ben's house with a uniformed officer within fifteen minutes of Ben's call. He grunted in response to Ben's greeting and spent several minutes in silence looking around the house.

"Did they take anything?" asked Townsend still pacing around the living room prodding stacks of books.

"Nothing that I'm aware of."

"Any real damage?"

"Not really," answered Ben.

"Doesn't really look like a prank. Seems like they were looking for something. What were they looking for?"

"I don't know. Don't have anything of real value. Could have been the final exam that happens tomorrow."

Detective Townsend thought for a moment.

"No, that doesn't make sense. They wouldn't have made this mess. If you knew they'd found it, you would have just changed the exam."

"I guess you're right," said Ben.

"What else could they've been looking for?"

"I've no idea."

"They seemed to have concentrated on your books. Do you have any valuable first editions? Anything like that?"

"No, not a one."

"Well, if you come up with anything, let me know. And sometime this afternoon, I'd like you to come down to the station to confirm and sign the report."

"The report?"

"That's right, the report of the break in. Just routine." As Detective Townsend left, he said, "By the way, they got in through the back door. You really shouldn't leave the key under the mat."

Murder

Ben started to restore his house to order, but soon realized that he had to shower and change quickly to meet Marie for lunch. Still puzzled by the meaning of the break in, he arrived at Marie's apartment door and knocked. No answer. She must not be back from her errands yet. He tried the door in hopes of waiting for her inside. It was open. He entered the apartment and froze in horror. Marie lay on the couch, the handle of a kitchen knife protruding from her chest. Marie was dead.

The grisly sight hit Ben like a punch in the stomach. Head down, he stumbled to his knees on the floor by the couch, unable to breathe. After a long moment, Ben reached up and touched her shoulder with the idea that, somehow, she might still be alive, but he found it cold. She had been dead for some time. He moved away from the couch and sank into a kitchen chair with his head in his hands. Who could have done this? And why? Marie. So beautiful. Such a lively spirit. Now dead. What a waste. Ben sat in shock for a full ten minutes before he realized that he needed to act.

Once again he called the police station and once again he met Detective Townsend at the door. This time Townsend's manner was not civil. Ben realized that he was definitely a suspect. Ben was told to sit in a chair and not to move until Townsend had finished his examination of the apartment. The apartment had been ransacked as well. Marie's body showed some bruises about the face and arms but was otherwise perfect, except for the knife and, of course, the pool of blood beneath her on the couch. Townsend spent only a short time looking at the body, leaving that task for the medical examiner. Ben had the feeling that Townsend was bothered by the sight of blood. Townsend pulled up a chair in front of Ben and began his interrogation.

"We'll go down to the station shortly, but first, I want to ask you a few questions while we're here."

Ben raised his head and faced Townsend.

"What can *I* tell you? I just walked in and found her."

"How do you know her?"

"We met last night at the Faculty Club cocktail party. She is Marie LaFontaine, a graduate student in the History Department."

"Why are you here?" asked Townsend.

"I came to take her to lunch. She asked for my help on a mathematical problem she's researching."

"Are you generally involved with students?"

"No, and we're not involved. Her advisor, George Rawlings, suggested that she ask for my help."

"Did you have sex with her?"

"No," answered Ben in protest, "I don't go around sleeping with students."

"She's been dead for some time. Were you here last night?"

"Yes, for dinner."

"Did you spend the night here?"

"No."

"You didn't spend it at home unless you did the ransacking yourself."

"No, I didn't sleep at home either," said Ben, "I slept on my boat at the marina."

"We can check that out. Are you ready to tell me what they, or you, were looking for?"

"I don't know what you're talking about," protested Ben.

Detective Townsend stood up and paced to the window and back to Ben.

"Well, here's the way it is. I have a ransacked house, a ransacked apartment, the dead body of a beautiful girl, and you, involved in all three incidents and probably the last person to see her alive."

"Except for the killer," said Ben, "except for the killer."

Townsend pondered Ben's reply for a good thirty seconds, long enough to make Ben feel very uncomfortable.

"Did you drive here, Professor?"

"Yes, my car's outside."

"Well, I'd like you to meet me at the police station in half an hour. Bring a lawyer if you wish. Plan to be there for a while."

"How long is *a while?*"

"We'll see how it goes. Somewhere between two hours and twenty years," Townsend said with a grim smile.

Alone in his car on the way to the police station, Ben had some tough decisions to make. He wanted to help the investigation in any way he could. *Almost* any way. He was not ready to admit to having slept with Marie, although if there were a DNA match found in the future, it would not go well for him. He tried to convince himself that there might not be any of his DNA left on the body. He decided that he would tell Townsend about the triangulation problem that Marie had presented but he would not mention that the text was still in his possession unless he had to. For some strange reason, he felt compelled to go over the text with George to see if it was somehow related to her death. In any case, he doubted that the police would ever figure it out on their own. He could always bring the text forward later claiming that he hadn't known that it was relevant. He decided not to involve a lawyer at this point. Yes, he was probably a suspect but it should be evident soon that he was not the killer.

In order to waste some time, Ben stopped for some coffee at a small shop on his way to the police station. Townsend had said

She Blew into the Room

half an hour and Ben didn't want to arrive too early. He found Detective Townsend in his office, a small, neat space with desk, desk chair, two filing cabinets, and a single visitor's chair. There was no room for anything else. Townsend pointed to the visitor's chair as he closed the blinds on the windows connecting his office and the rest of the police station. The room darkened considerably. It could have been a scene from one of the old cops/robbers movies except that Townsend didn't smoke.

Turning on a tape recorder on his desk Townsend remarked, "I assume that you don't object."

"No objection."

"And you're not bringing in a lawyer?"

"Not at this point."

Townsend settled in behind his desk, "Let's go back to when you met Marie, you said, for the first time."

"Right, it was at the Faculty Club cocktail party. She came in toward the end, soaked from the rain shower."

"And you picked her up?"

"Nobody picked up anybody."

"How did you meet?"

"She got a drink and walked directly over to me."

"You said that you had never met, how did she know who you were?"

"I mentioned before that she was a graduate student of George Rawlings in the History Department. He suggested that she contact me and he gave her my description."

"Interesting," said the detective, "and how did she know where you were?"

"Free drinks and all that," said Ben, already sorry for the flippant answer.

"What did you say?"

"George guessed that I would be at the faculty cocktail because of the *free drinks and all that*."

"And he was right."

"Yes, he was right."

"Then what happened?"

"She told me that she needed someone with a mathematical mind to look at a problem in a 17th century text that she was working on."

"And that's what you have?"

"What I have?"

"A mathematical mind, Professor."

"I would hope so since I'm a professor in the Math Department."

"Yes, one would hope. Then what happened?"

"She offered me dinner if I would look at her problem."

"Is that how you ended up at her apartment?"

"Yes, she was drenched. We went there so she could change and make dinner."

"Sounds great. Candle-lit dinner with a beautiful foreign student."

"It was all very professional, Detective."

"I'm sure. I'm sure. Did she live alone?"

"Yes, I think so, although there was a young man sleeping on the couch when we arrived."

"What was his name?"

"I don't know. She didn't introduce us. She said something to him in French and he left. When I asked about him she said that he was a *temporary flat mate* and that he had something that he needed to do."

"What did he look like, this *temporary flat mate*?"

"Young, dark, medium height."

"And…"

"And what? That's about all I can say about him?"

"Young, dark, medium height describes half the male population of this town. What else can you tell me?"

"I don't know. I only saw him for a minute."

"How young?"

"Less than thirty."

"You think he was French?"

"Well, she spoke to him in French."

"How dark was he?"

"Pretty dark. Come to think of it, I don't think that he was Northern European."

"From where, then?"

"I don't know, he looked more like an Arab, sort of."

Townsend stood up and started to pace. Unfortunately, the small office provided little pacing room and every pass the detective made next to Ben's chair gave Ben a menacing feeling.

"Okay, Professor, we have a less than thirty, pretty dark, sort of Arab, maybe French-speaking, *temporary flat mate* of medium height who was in her apartment the evening of her death."

"That's about it," said Ben. "Sorry."

"Well, *sorry* doesn't cut it," said Townsend as he sat back down.

After a long pause the detective asked, "And then what?"

"Well, while she was cooking, she described her problem that had to do with this 17th century French text she was working on. It involved a technique called triangulation, the method they used to create an accurate map of France for Louis XIV."

"And you solved her problem?"

"Well…yes… I pointed out something she didn't know about the French using Paris for the prime meridian and that seemed to resolve her issue."

"So, just like that, you earned your dinner."

"Yes, just my dinner." Ben flushed as he remembered how the grateful Marie had taken him to bed."

"And then what?"

"She made an excited phone call to someone in French and we had dinner."

"What was the call about?"

"I don't know. Don't really understand French that well and I wasn't trying to listen, but I assume that it was about the solution to her problem."

"How long was the call?"

"Very short. Twenty seconds, max."

"Land line or mobile."

"Land line because I can remember the old dial phone they had in the apartment."

"Good. Did she have to look up the number?"

Ben paused, "No, I remember that she dialed it from memory. You know, you might check the phone records."

At this, Townsend exploded and left the room muttering something about meddling professors; of course they would check the phone records. While out of the room Townsend got reports from his subordinates. Evidently, the night watchman at the marina had confirmed Ben's story as had some of the attendees of the cocktail party.

The detective reentered his office and resumed the interrogation.

"Okay, she made the phone call, you had dinner, then what?"

"That's about it. We shared a bottle of wine. Celebration, you know. She had been struggling with that problem for quite some time. We talked for a long time. And then I left."

"What time did you leave?"

Ben had been dreading this question. After sex, sleep, and shower he probably didn't leave Marie's apartment until midnight or later, he couldn't remember. How was he going to square this with Townsend without telling him the whole truth? The night watchman at the marina might have noted when he arrived. *Have to assume so.* Saying that he had left at eight to go home before going to the boat could blow up in his face since it might be shown that the break-in at his house occurred earlier than he thought. *Have to take that chance. If you're going to tell a lie, stick as close to the truth as you can.*

"I don't know. It was late."

"How late?"

"I really don't know. As I said, we shared a bottle of wine and talked for a long time. Ten, maybe. I left around ten and stopped by my house before going down to the boat."

Townsend pondered for a moment, "The night watchman at the marina said you rolled in around twelve thirty."

"Really, that late?"

"Yes, you must have stopped by your house for two hours or so."

"I don't know. It didn't seem that long."

Townsend said nothing, waiting for more explanation. Ben decided to remain silent. The impasse was finally broken by the detective.

"And why did you show up at her apartment this afternoon?"

"I had offered to take her out to lunch."

"And found her dead."

"Did you touch anything? Change anything?"

"No, well…I touched her to see if she might be alive. Stupid, I know, with a knife in her chest, but I suppose I was in shock. I sat for a bit, then phoned you."

During the following two hours Detective Townsend went over Ben's story again and again. The missing hours between Ben's alleged departure from Marie's apartment and his arrival at the marina seemed to be a major sticking point. Ben was sinking lower in his chair, feeling guilty of almost everything except killing Marie. Finally, they both were tired enough to quit.

Townsend sat up straight and looked Ben in the eye. "I'm going to release you. There's not enough evidence to book you *yet*. Stay in the area until further notice. I *will* want to talk to you again."

Ben drove to the university, left his car in his labeled spot, and walked across the commons to the History Department and George's office. George had just finished a conversation with one of his graduate students. He ushered Ben into his office. His face was ashen.

"We've had a terrible tragedy," George said. "One of our graduate students was killed last night."

"Yes, I know. Marie LaFontaine."

"How did you know?" asked George, somewhat surprised.

"I found the body."

"Oh, my god. So she *did* contact you about her triangulation problem." George got up and closed his office door.

"Yes, we talked about it last night, had dinner at her apartment, and may have solved the problem."

"But...when did you find her body?"

"When I stopped by today to return the text and take her to lunch."

"The French text? You still have the text?"

"George, you have to level with me. What's this all about? Could the text have been important enough to get her killed?"

"Do you still have the text?" George's insistence startled Ben.

"Yes, I have it in a safe place. I didn't mention it to the police, who, by the way have been interrogating me all afternoon."

"Do the police think that you killed her?" asked George.

"I'm the prime suspect at the moment. And if there is a DNA match later, then I'm in real trouble."

"What, you slept with her?" George practically shouted.

"I'm sorry. A moment of passion. You knew her. She was very persuasive. Could you have resisted her?"

"Never had the opportunity," mumbled George.

They sat silent for a while.

"Now that I've answered your questions, George, it's your turn to answer mine. What was she working on? Why would the text be important enough to someone to kill for it?"

"I don't know if it *is* important enough. I can tell you what she thought she knew. But it's a long story and I need to get out of here and have a drink first. This thing is such a mess. If it's true that the text was the reason for her murder, then we have some mad men on the loose and you, my friend, are in great danger."

"I've considered that."

"Get the text, make sure that you're not being followed, and come to my house for drinks and dinner. I'll tell you all I know. God, I can't believe it. I just can't believe it."

Ben followed his instructions. He avoided the temptation to return home. There was no need to since the text was still under the passenger seat of his car. His original intuition about the importance of the text returned to nag him. And George had been insistent about learning if Ben still had the text so George must think it's important too. What if the killers had been looking for the text in his house? What if Marie had given him the text knowing that someone dangerous would come looking for it? After searching for the text in her apartment, perhaps the killers had forced her to tell them who had the text. Finding out where he lived in this small town wouldn't have taken five minutes. She knew that he had a boat from their dinner conversation, but she wouldn't have known that he would choose to spend the night on the boat. He hadn't made that decision until he was in his car after leaving her apartment early that morning.

He drove down isolated roads, turned around, waited, and retraced his path to ensure that he wasn't being followed. Then he made his way to the Rawlings' house and parked in back out of sight.

George Rawlings' house was somewhat above the level of the average professor's house. George had married well and his wife, Frieda, supplemented their academic income substantially through her trust fund. Perhaps *supplemented* was not the right word. In any case George was an academic simply because that's what he chose to be.

Ben retrieved the text from under the car seat and walked towards the kitchen entrance. Frieda Rawlings met Ben at the door, looking gracious and elegant as always. She gave Ben a kiss on the cheek and ushered him inside.

"Do you think that you were followed?" she asked. Evidently Frieda shared George's concern that Ben was somehow in danger.

"No, I doubled back and did all the spy things," Ben said after some consideration. He caught himself trying to make light of the situation and realized that he was still in shock from the day's events. Marie's murder was just beginning to establish itself as a reality. A ghastly, grim reality. And, yet, the problem-solving part of his brain would not let go of the puzzle. *Why was she killed? What did the text and her triangulation problem have to do with her death? Would George know what was going on?* He couldn't turn off his brain.

"What's for dinner?" he asked.

"Squab in Dijon butter."

Ben smiled. Nothing simple or ordinary from Frieda. Ben had always assumed that she was a product of the German aristocracy although he had never felt comfortable enough to find out for sure. Frieda ushered Ben into the study where George was making a batch of Martinis. From George's condition it was clear to Ben that this was not the first batch of the day. As if reading Ben's mind, George said, "It's not every day that one of my graduate students gets murdered."

They raised their glasses.

"Here's to Marie," said Ben. "And I hope that they catch her killer."

They drank in silence, no one knowing what to say. Finally, Frieda left the study to look after dinner. Ben placed the text in front of George and asked, "Now, can you tell me what you know of her studies? I've only glanced through the text, but it looks like poetry of some kind."

"It *is* poetry. French baroque poetry to be precise. Written by a mediocre poet and adventurer by the name of François Gerard."

"How could his poetry have anything to do with her death?"

George poured another drink for both of them.

"Sit down. It's a long story."

George opened the text and placed his hand on the title page as if to establish the reference. It struck Ben that he must be completely familiar with its contents.

"François Gerard grew up in France/Bavaria during the latter part of the Thirty Years War. Sometimes a soldier, he found himself in the service of the Duke of Lorraine. After the Peace of Westphalia—"

"When was that?"

"1648…After the Peace, things were still understandably chaotic in the area. We know that Gerard was still around Besançon which was ceded to France in 1678. We know that he was loaned to Picard in 1679 to work on the triangulation survey of France commissioned by Louis XIV. Some time around 1680, Gerard was sent, probably by the duke, on a mission to sack a chateau near Besançon. He was in charge of a small force that was successful in relieving the chateau of a treasure that had been accumulated during the previous wars."

"But, what—"

"Hang on, it gets better. On the way back to the duke, Gerard's force was supposedly attacked and overwhelmed. Only Gerard survived and the treasure mysteriously disappeared."

"And the duke was unhappy—"

"To say the least. The duke threw Gerard into his dungeon where he spent the last four years of his life. That's where he wrote the poetry that we have here."

"And the treasure?"

"The treasure never resurfaced as far as we know."

"But how was Marie's work related to the treasure?"

George settled back in his chair and lowered his voice. "She believed, like the duke, that Gerard had hidden the treasure, that he finally realized that he was never going to be released, and that he embedded clues of the location of the treasure in his poetry as a parting gesture of defiance against the duke."

"That seems to be quite a stretch."

"I know, but I think that she might have been right," said George, returning to his drink.

"George, why did she come all the way to New England to enlist your help?"

George looked down and moved uneasily in his chair. "During the Baroque period there was an evolution in poetry styles, especially in France. Traditional meters changed. Rhyming took on a series of inventive forms."

"Rhyming?"

"Yes, instead of rhyming in couplets as in a simple poem or in pairs of couplets mixed in stanzas of four verses, the rhyme or, more importantly, the connection between ideas might be distributed across stanzas themselves. Always with a definite pattern, to be sure, but sometimes in complex forms."

"But why—"

"To allow the beautiful expression of complex thoughts."

"And that is your world-famous specialty?"

"Well, anyway, the history of the evolution. Otherwise I would have ended up in a literature department somewhere."

"But why was that so important in understanding the Gerard text?"

"Because, Marie believed, that Gerard used the same device to hide the clues to the whereabouts of the treasure. He embedded the clues throughout the text. To find them she needed to identify the pattern that he devised. I was the logical choice."

"Did you find the pattern?"

"Yes, after struggling with it for over a month, I think that we cracked it."

"Then the problem was solved."

"Hardly. She then had to apply the pattern to the text to find out where the clues were embedded. A difficult piece of work, but I think that she figured it out."

"Who else knew what she was working on?"

"In detail, just me, as far as I know. Well, with the possible exception of her sister, Thérèse. Never met her. A twin, I seem to recall."

"Yes, Marie told me about her last night," said Ben.

"Thérèse works for a small investment firm somewhere in France. A fairly questionable firm as far as Frieda could find out.

Anyway, Thérèse got Marie interested in the Gerard affair in the first place. Marie had worked on it on her own for a while at the Sorbonne before she asked me to take her on as one of my graduate students. So maybe some people there knew what she was doing."

"I see. So it wasn't a complete secret."

"Well, that's part of my problem with all this. I might have mentioned it to the wrong people and bear some responsibility for her death."

"Don't beat yourself up on that account. As you said the Sorbonne might have been a source of information for the wrong people. And, when Marie and I made the breakthrough last night, she called someone and told them about it."

"Who did she call?"

"I don't know. All I know is that she spoke to them in French."

Frieda entered the study to announce dinner. "Did I hear my name taken?" she asked.

"Yes, what was the name of that investment firm that Marie's sister works for?"

"Bonsans, Bonjans, or something like that. In any case, my investment banker friends seemed to think that it was just a front for private money, possibly a laundering operation. Why do you want to know?"

"Ben was trying to determine who else knew about Marie's work."

"Just us," said Frieda. "Dinner's ready."

Frieda's cooking was excellent as usual but she seemed to be the only one with much of an appetite. George had opened a bottle of Châteauneuf-du-Pape for the table but continued to drink Martinis. The dinner conversation lagged giving Ben time to put his thoughts in order. He needed to find a quiet, safe place to think things through. And for that, there was no place better than his boat. By the time dessert arrived, he had decided to go for a short sail up the Maine coast. Townsend had told him not to leave the area, but Maine might be considered more or less the same area. Well, perhaps not. Anyway he would give Townsend a call once at sea and let him know where he was. No use stirring things up unnecessarily.

After dinner, George went over the sections of the text that Marie had identified as being potential clues to the location of the treasure. George claimed that he didn't understand how she had managed to determine a position in latitude/longitude terms. Thanking his hosts, Ben left, taking the text with him. George's inclination had been to keep it, but, as Frieda pointed out, the text might be material evidence in a murder case and if Ben wanted to hold onto it, they shouldn't interfere.

Ben arranged to borrow George's car to make a quick stop at home to pick up a few things he would need for the trip. He parked on the next block and entered his house through the back door. He bundled up his sailing gear, some food and wine and drove down to the marina. George would switch cars in the morning. Safer, they all had thought.

Flight

Once aboard *Emma*, Ben started to regain his composure. He thought of Hemmingway's depiction of a bull finding its *estancia* in the bull ring—the place where the bull felt comfortable and became more powerful. His cutter, *Emma*, was his *estancia*. A few days of sailing and he would work everything out. Logic would prevail.

The only troublesome item was the fact that he found the companionway hatch closed but unlocked. Nothing was disturbed below so it did not cause him much concern. He examined the lock and found it undamaged. Perhaps he had forgotten to lock up when he left in the morning.

He started up the engine, a vintage, two-cylinder diesel engine that made more of a rumble than a roar. Navigation lights on, he slipped his mooring lines and quietly motored out of the peaceful harbor. At night, early in the season, he had the sea to himself. There was just enough moonlight to pick his way through the field of lobster trap floats. Once into deeper water, he raised the mainsail, unfurled the genoa, and set the autopilot on a course Down East. The wind was northwest at 12 knots. Couldn't have been more cooperative.

Ben went below and opened a bottle of wine. He was about to return to the cockpit when he heard a rustling noise from the forward cabin. He opened the cabin door and switched on the light. He dropped the wine and almost lost consciousness. There, peering at him from behind a sail bag, was the face of the girl he had found dead just hours before. She was very much alive.

"Marie...what the—"

"No Marie. Thérèse," came the halting reply. "I am Thérèse, sister of Marie."

Ben picked up the wine bottle and tried to control his emotions. Except for shorter and darker hair, the woman before him was an exact copy of Marie.

"Sorry I surprise you. Please forgive. Marie is dead. Maybe I be dead too. No place to go. Sorry."

Her English was broken with a strong French accent. Ben couldn't take his eyes from her. He had to keep reminding himself that Marie was dead. This was not Marie. This was not Marie. Ben slumped onto the settee, still holding the bottle of wine. Thérèse entered the main cabin and placed a hand on Ben's shoulder.

"You love Marie?" she asked.

"No, we just met..." He shook his head, "Well, yes, I suppose that I do...did love her in a way."

"I am sorry," she said giving Ben a caress on his cheek. She took two non-skid rocks glasses from the rack in the galley and waited for Ben to pour.

"We are alone?" she asked.

"Yes."

"Where we go?"

"Maine for a few days."

"*Magnifique*. Who know where we go?"

"Nobody really. We would be hard to find."

"*Bon*. You have food? I have great hunger."

Thérèse's apparent composure bothered and perplexed Ben. She looked sad and her eyes showed signs of crying, but one would never guess from her demeanor that her sister had just been murdered. Perhaps she mourned privately. Perhaps she had not been that close to her sister even though they were twins. In any case, Ben produced some cold cuts, bread and cheese which Thérèse devoured rapidly, paying little attention to Ben or her surroundings. Ben watched her, still reminding himself that she was not Marie.

She was dressed in jeans and a light silk blouse, hardly sufficient for an early season night sail. After directing Thérèse to his clothes locker, he refilled his wine glass and returned to the cockpit. He was on watch, after all. And he needed time to think.

The night was clear and cool. The offshore wind produced little in the way of waves and *Emma* was moving well. Maine by morning, he thought. He zipped up his jacket and sat facing the wind. It helped clear the cobwebs. Now he could start to figure things out. In all likelihood, Thérèse was in danger from the people who killed her sister. Perhaps he was as well, although he still had difficulty believing that part. But how was Thérèse involved in the Francois Gerard text? George had told him that she, at least, knew about it, and had suggested it to Marie. Why did she show up in New England the very day that her sister was killed? Coincidence? Not likely. Perhaps she was the person that Marie had called when the longitude problem had been solved. If so, and if she had been in France, she couldn't have arrived here before Marie was killed. Unless she was already here. Thérèse must have had contact with Marie before she died. How else could she have known about Ben? How else could she have chosen his boat as a hiding place? And if she had made contact, what part did she play in her sister's murder? No, he couldn't believe that this girl could have killed her sister. Nothing made sense. He realized that he was sinking deeper and deeper into confusion.

Thérèse joined him in the cockpit, bundled in a heavy sweater and windbreaker and carrying her glass and the bottle of wine. She refilled his glass and sat next to him without comment. They sat in silence for awhile and listened to the gurgling of the sea around the hull. Ben had a dozen questions for her, but didn't know how or where to start. Thérèse saved him the trouble.

"You have questions for me?" she asked.

"A few. Like, when did you last talk to Marie?"

"Early this morning."

"In person?"

"I not understand."

"Did you talk to her by phone or were you at the apartment?"

"Oh, in person at the apartment. A hour after you left."

"After I left? How do you know when I left?"

"I see you. I arrive when you leave. Marie at the window. I think you are other person so I follow you. You go to this boat, the *Emma* boat. I see you are not the person. I go back to Marie."

"Who did you think I was?" asked Ben after a moment.

"Nobody. Not important."

Ben didn't agree that it was not important, but the look on Thérèse's face in the half light told him that he was not going to find out tonight.

"Then you went back to the apartment?" he asked.

"Yes."

"And then what?'

"We talk. Long time apart, you know. We have good time. She talk about you. Then, we talk about other things and we fight. Not bad fight. Just argue. And I leave."

"What did you fight about?"

"Not important."

"Please, Thérèse, it may be important."

Thérèse considered the question for awhile.

"You know the book of Francois Gerard?" she asked quietly. "My company want to know what she discovers. She refuse. We fight. I leave."

"And that was the last time you saw her alive?"

Thérèse bolted away from Ben, spilling her wine, and sat on the other side of the cockpit facing him. Her violent reaction surprised him.

Flight

"I'm sorry," he said, "I didn't mean—"

"Someone kill her. And they will try to kill me," she said as she dissolved in tears, burying her face in her knees.

Ben placed his hand on the back of her head in a clumsy effort to comfort her. She sobbed and he felt like a fool. A first class fool. The rest of his questions would have to wait. He quickly put together a possible chain of events. Thérèse later returned to the apartment, found Marie dead, panicked, and fled to the boat to hide. Possible. Even believable.

They sailed on without further conversation. Thérèse stopped sobbing and eventually moved back beside Ben and curled up with her head on his shoulder for a while. Ben found the intimacy surprising but didn't complain. Then she evidently decided that she couldn't sleep in the cockpit and went below without comment. Ben was perplexed. His faith in his abilities to logically work out the solution to almost any puzzle was starting to crumble. The more he learned about the events surrounding Marie's death, the more he became stymied. It would be safe to say that he was making no progress. None at all.

Ben scanned the familiar lights on shore. He had made the trip down to Maine many times and could probably make it safely without GPS. Out to sea, he could see two ships headed for Boston, but they were well offshore. In a few hours *Emma* would be crossing the shipping lanes for the traffic moving to and from Portland and the south, but, for now they were alone. Ben reached inside the cabin for the pen light that he kept on a shelf next to the companionway. He found his cell phone and the card that Townsend had given him. Best to check in, or out, before we get out of cell phone range. After two rings, Townsend answered.

"Detective Townsend."

"Sorry to call so late. This is Ben Slade and I just wanted to let you know that I have gone out for a sail."

There was a pause.

"You're not supposed to leave the area."

"I'm close by and you now have my cell number if you need to talk to me. Besides, I think that whoever killed Marie might be looking for me."

"Why do you think that?" asked Townsend.

"I was with her before she was killed. They were looking for something at her place and at my house."

"If they're looking for you, we can protect you."

"Thanks, but I think that I'm safer where I am."

"Where are you, exactly?"

Ben covered the cell phone with the sleeve of his foul weather jacket. "Sorry, Detective Townsend, the connection seems to be breaking up. I'll call you in the morning when I'm closer to land," said Ben as he hit the End button on his phone. He was ashamed of his adolescent manner of terminating his call with Townsend, but he was not willing to discuss or divulge more at the moment.

Detective Townsend, far from being disturbed, was mildly amused by the call. He knew that he could locate Ben if he had to, as long as Ben kept his cell phone on. And the fact that Ben felt the need to check in made his story more credible. The "bad connection" ruse only confirmed his suspicion that Ben was withholding information. Had the detective known just how much information Ben was withholding, he would have been furious.

Ben spent the next few hours musing in the cockpit between periods of avoiding Portland shipping traffic. It became clear that, at some point, he would have to tell Townsend everything. The Gerard text. Thérèse's involvement. Maybe even his relationship with Marie. But not now. He had to get things clear in his mind first. Right before dawn, he ducked below to make some coffee. Settled again in the cockpit, he took part in one of his favorite experiences in sailing—watching the sunrise on a crystal clear morning. Thérèse joined him, warming her hands on her coffee mug. The first thing she saw was a large freighter about to cross their path not one hundred yards away.

"He see us?" she asked.

"If the officer on watch isn't doing the sparks," said Ben with a laugh.

"What is sparks?"

"Well, it's a long story but I guess we've got plenty of time. I was a post graduate student in London for a year during which time I bought a sports car for export back to the United States. So when the year was up I booked passage for the car and myself on a Norwegian freighter bound for Baltimore. I traveled 'supercargo', one of only two passengers on the ship. We had meals with the captain and officers and got to know them quite well during the ten-day voyage. Norwegians have a strange, but well developed, sense of humor. The sparks, or radio operator, was a young attractive Norwegian woman whose cabin was on the bridge deck near the radio equipment. There was a small lounge on the next deck below the bridge deck where Captain Bull and I would often meet in the evening to drink his cognac and listen to his sea stories. He had been in the merchant marine during the war and had enough sea stories to last all the way across the Atlantic."

"Yes, a long story," she said.

"Anyway, one night we were passing through a storm, not dangerous for a ship that size, but uncomfortable. The captain paused in his story-telling to phone the bridge to check with the second officer who was on watch. The phone rang and rang. And the longer it rang, the angrier the captain became. The captain was not about to give up and after what seemed like several minutes the phone was finally answered. Some harsh Norwegian words were spoken. I didn't have to understand them to know that the second officer's maritime career was in jeopardy. It seemed that he had left his post at the bridge to do some sparking with the sparks."

"Poor man," said Thérèse.

"So every time I see an approaching freighter I don't assume that they see us. I wonder if the officer on watch has found something more interesting to do."

Ben smiled at her.

"So you found the coffee," he said.

"The odor woke me. Good coffee."

"Thanks. You seem to be comfortable on a boat," he said, in part trying to make up for the night before.

"We are from Bandol. South coast. Girls from Bandol know boats," she said with some pride.

"You seem to know them quite well. Did you sleep okay?"

"Well, thank you. But you were awake all night?"

Ben involuntarily stretched his shoulder muscles as he was starting to feel the effects of his all-night vigil. "I'll get a chance to sleep soon," he said as he pointed to a small island appearing next to the sun in the distance before them.

"Damariscove," he said as if it were important.

"We anchor there?"

"Sort of. More like tying up. You'll see."

Thérèse didn't respond and they silently watched the sun move higher and the island grow larger. An hour later they approached an inlet on the south side of the island. A slit in the rock, really. Ben had Thérèse take the helm as he dropped the sails. She was competent enough to be sure. Then Ben took over to steer through the slit which served as the entrance. There was little surf which made their passage relatively easy. Ben could remember the first time he came in here, heart in his mouth, with rocky shore close on both sides of the inlet. Inside, the harbor didn't open up much at all. The sailing guide featured a picture of the island from the nineteenth century, filled with several fishing schooners two or three times *Emma's* size. All rafted up and packing the narrow harbor from shore to shore. The refuge was empty now, except for a small unmanned park service vessel tied up at the head of the harbor. Ben turned *Emma* around, backing and filling in order to complete the turn. How the schooners had done it, he had no idea. He moved back up the inlet toward the ocean, dropped anchor, and backed down toward a stone protrusion into the harbor which must have served as a dock a century ago. Thérèse was ahead of his commands, preparing a line at *Emma's* stern to pass through one of the large iron rings left in the dock by sailors long past. Ben tightened the anchor chain. *Emma* was snuggly moored with rock walls on either side. He smiled at Thérèse.

"Just like mooring in the south of France," he said.

"Yes, just like. Now, sleep."

Ben didn't need to be told twice. He went below and curled up in the forward cabin. *Emma's* gentle motion in the protected harbor helped him fall into a deep sleep almost immediately. The tension and the stress of the past twenty-four hours seemed to wash away.

Around noon he awoke with a start. For a few moments he couldn't remember where he was or why. The familiar surroundings of *Emma's* cabin brought him to the present. The smell of the ocean air reminded him that he was in Maine. Reality took a little longer. He revisited the previous day's events. The break-in. Marie's death. Townsend's suspicions. Then it struck him. Marie's sister, Thérèse, was onboard. Where was she? He pulled on his sweater and headed up the companionway. The day was crisp as befits Maine in the spring, but the high rocks around the harbor protected them from the wind. He found Thérèse sitting on the foredeck staring off into space. He sat beside her but she hardly acknowledged his presence.

"I'm very sorry about your sister," he said.

She turned her gaze toward him. "I, as well. I want the killers to die."

"Do you have any idea who might be responsible?"

"Some idea."

"Does it have to do with the Gerard text?"

"Yes."

Ben thought for a moment. As much as he wished otherwise, he was involved in the whole affair. And, sooner or later, he would have to return home. Hiding from the killers was not a long term option.

"We should go to the police," he said.

"No, not police," she said with some force.

"Why not?"

"No police."

"Well, we can't stay here forever."

"How long?"

Ben was surprised at the question. "A few days," he said. "A little longer if we can catch some fish."

"Then we catch fish. First some lunch. Hungry?"

Thérèse jumped up and went below. Ben could hear her rummaging through the fridge and lockers in search of material for lunch. Once again, he was amazed at Thérèse's ability to put tragedy aside and to move on as if nothing had happened. Something about not being able to change the past, he mused, only the present and maybe the future. Thérèse's vehement desire to avoid the police troubled him. He knew that, sooner or later, they would have no choice but to tell Townsend everything. After a few minutes, he went below to help, noting that Thérèse had the same effect on him that her sister had had. He was confused, three steps behind, and trying to catch up. And he didn't mind.

After lunch, Ben produced a tackle box and a spinning rod. Thérèse helped him lower the dinghy over the side. He offered to go with her but she was adamant about going alone. He watched her row out of the inlet.

"Girls from Bandol know boats," he repeated to himself.

While Thérèse was out looking for their dinner, Ben took the opportunity to assess their situation. *Emma* was in good shape, having just been launched. Water and fuel tanks were full. Batteries in good shape. The only incomplete repair he could think of was the radar reflector. *Emma* had been stored on the hard with the mast in place. A winter storm had detached the radar reflector from the rigging and the fall had bent it out of shape. Ben had bought a replacement but had not had time to install it. Now that they were in foggy Maine, a radar reflector was required, especially since *Emma's* wooden spars did little to give other vessels any indication of their presence. He retrieved the new reflector from the lazarette and hoisted it to the spreader on the port flag halyard. Not a permanent solution, but workable for the time being.

Thérèse returned within the hour with a two-pound flounder. She held it up for Ben to see and simply said, "*Une limande.*" Ben didn't feel that it was appropriate to ask her how she had done it, but the bits of broken shells and sand in the bottom of the dinghy suggested that she had been jigging with clams. With the flounder cleaned and placed in the fridge, they used the dinghy to reach the landing, some ten feet away, and began exploring the island.

She Blew into the Room

The island, indeed, was deserted except for birds. There were a few out-buildings, a one-room museum, and a disused lifeboat station. Ben and Thérèse strolled the island with little comment, covering the southern part of the island in an hour. The northern part of the island was reserved as a breeding ground for common eiders which return to the island each spring. They stood at the barrier to the breeding ground and watched the nesting activity for some time. For some reason, perhaps because of the teacher in him, Ben felt the need to add a bit of history to their afternoon.

"This island was one of the earliest European settlement sites in the New World. In the 1600's, before Jamestown or Plymouth. The fishing was so good here that it drew fishing fleets from Portugal and Northern Europe. That tiny harbor that we're in has seen a lot of traffic."

"Now all gone. Almost sad," she said.

"At least the island has been returned to the birds."

They returned to *Emma* and Ben climbed into the forward berth for a short nap. Getting too old for all-nighters, he thought. He was awakened by the hiss of the kettle as it started to boil. Thérèse was at the sink, filling a basin with water for a sponge bath. The small hot water tank, which was heated by the engine, had long gone cold so the kettle and sponge bath provided the only civilized option. Ben watched her through the open cabin door as she removed her clothes. She did not acknowledge his presence and made no attempt to hide from his view. There, before him, was the body that had captivated him two nights before. At least, it was a carbon copy of that memorable body. With one small exception. On her abdomen, just above the bikini line, was a small tattoo of a black butterfly. Ben couldn't take his eyes off of it.

Ben waited for her to finish dressing before he stirred.

"I'm sorry that the accommodations are so Spartan," he said.

Flight

"Not so Spartan, as you say. You have your *Emma* boat a long time?"

"Well, yes and no. My father and I found this boat abandoned in the corner of a Boston boatyard when I was still in junior high school. She was in bad shape. Fixing her up was sort of our father/son bonding project. Then we learned how to sail her together. Since my father was a teacher we had the summers to take some great trips. Up here to Maine and beyond to the Maritimes, down south to Nantucket and Martha's Vineyard. As far as the Chesapeake Bay one summer."

"Just you and your father?"

"Yes, my mother died when I was young and I have no siblings. Anyway, I went off to college and my father continued to sail *Emma* up until he died three years ago. That was about the time that I was coming back to New England so *Emma* was passed down to me."

"I love your *Emma* boat."

"I'm pleased that you do. Some wine, Thérèse?"

"*Toujours*," she replied.

Ben found a bottle of Sauvignon Blanc while Thérèse set about preparing the flounder for dinner. Baked flounder with capers and tomatoes. Some wild rice completed the meal. Thérèse knew how to cook.

After dinner they sat in the cockpit to enjoy the last of the wine and the last of the daylight. The daylight was fading fast as a heavy fog began rolling across the island. A moderate wind brought the fog over them in an instant.

"Glad that we're tied up in here tonight," he said, "it's getting pretty soupy out there."

Thérèse held her finger to her lips. There was a not-so-distant growl of a powerful motor boat. It wasn't entering their harbor, perhaps exploring the shore somewhere farther down the island. The sound stopped.

"Strange," said Ben, "most people wouldn't plan to arrive here at dusk. And if they knew anything about the island, they would head for this harbor."

They sat sipping their wine without comment. Both were wondering if, somehow, they had been pursued to this desolate spot. Impossible. No one knew where they were going. Only a handful knew that Ben was on the boat. A dark figure appeared on the rocks at the head of the harbor, some fifty yards away. He was talking to someone they couldn't see. And he obviously didn't realize that the wind at his back carried his voice down the boulder-lined harbor to *Emma*.

"There's his boat," sounded the voice in a low tone.

A chill went up Ben's spine. Thérèse grabbed his arm. They made no other movement or sound. It was possible that the new arrivals couldn't see them in the cockpit as *Emma* was completely dark.

Another voice responded, "Let's bring our boat around to make sure he doesn't get away."

The figure disappeared. Without a word, Ben and Thérèse sprang into action. Within seconds, Thérèse let go the stern mooring line while Ben started the engine and began raising the anchor. Thérèse took the helm while Ben finished securing the anchor onboard. She expertly navigated the narrow entrance and *Emma* was out to sea. On his way aft Ben lowered the radar reflector and signaled Thérèse to go upwind while he raised the mainsail. He returned to the cockpit, unfurled the genoa, shut off the engine, and put *Emma* on a southeast heading.

Thérèse looked at him as if to ask why, but said nothing.

"We're in stealth mode," he whispered. "No sound. No lights. Hardly a radar reflection. You've got to love these old wooden boats."

Flight

They could hear their pursuers' power boat engine starting up. Through the dense fog they could see a glow from the power boat's search light as they tried to find the narrow entrance to the harbor. Evidently successful, the glow disappeared into the slit in the rocks only to reappear a minute later, accompanied by the roar of the engine at high revs.

"Must have been a disappointment to find us gone," said Ben in a low voice.

"Do you think they will discover us?" asked Thérèse.

"We'll have to wait and see. Their search light won't do them much good in this fog. So much reflection that it's blinding. And there is no light coming from us."

Now well clear of the island, Ben altered course to the east and trimmed the sails. Their pursuers roared back and forth in an erratic search pattern, sometimes coming close enough for Ben to see the glow of the search light, but usually well out of range. The sound of the power boat's engine, however, was always in evidence. In the small waves *Emma* bounded forward at six knots in total darkness. Thérèse strained to see where they were going, but the effort was futile.

"They can't see us, but no one else can either," she said.

"We'll have to take that chance."

After ten minutes, Ben noticed that the engine roar was starting to get louder, much louder than it had been up to that point. He could see the glow of the search light getting brighter and brighter. As he glanced forward, he saw another dim glow, this one less than thirty yards away. Suddenly, out of the fog, a trawler appeared in their path. Thérèse gave a muffled shriek. Ben put the helm down, narrowly avoiding a collision. They were close enough to see the disgusted face of the trawler's captain in the dim illumination provided by the trawler's navigation lights.

"A light or two wouldn't hurt none. You ain't out for a fucking Sunday sail," came the rejoinder from the trawler.

A responsible sailor for all of his life, Ben felt the need to apologize but kept silent. He returned to his easterly course and listened to the increasing roar of the power boat. A minute later the power boat glanced off the hull of the trawler and entangled itself in the trawler's dredge cables. From *Emma* they could see nothing but the glow of the lights. However, the commotion was deafening as the trawler captain exercised some foul language that Ben hadn't heard since he spent a summer on a fishing boat during his undergraduate years. *Emma* continued her course away from the scene.

"What luck," said Thérèse.

"Luck for sure," said Ben. "The power boat probably picked up the trawler on their radar, thought it was *Emma*, and headed right for her."

Thérèse was silent for a moment, then asked, "Who do you think they were?"

"I don't know. Marie's killers, I would assume. But I can't understand how they knew where to look for us. A GPS transmitter hidden on *Emma* doesn't make sense. They would have found us easily in the fog if they would have had one. Besides, only three people knew that I was on the boat, unless someone saw us leave the marina. Even with that, only a few of my friends know that I like to come to that island."

That thought occupied Ben for a while. In past seasons, he had sailed to Damariscove a few times with various guests—a couple of graduate students, some sailing club friends, and others, including George and Frieda Rawlings. Ben went over the list in his mind, rejecting the suggestion that any of those people could be connected to Marie's brutal death. But the enigma remained. Someone knew

Flight

Ben well enough to guess correctly where he would make his first stop.

They sailed on through the dense black fog. Ben kept watching the glow behind them get dimmer. From time to time, Ben would switch on his radar to get a glimpse of potential traffic, but for the rest of the time they sailed silent and dark. Finally, after an hour of total darkness, he felt it safe to turn on his masthead light. He usually didn't run with his navigation lights since they interfered with his night vision. Especially with such a heavy fog. He put the coordinates of Mistake Island into the GPS as a waypoint and adjusted his heading to ENE.

"Where we go?" asked Thérèse.

"Mistake Island, and I hope it's not."

Thérèse looked puzzled, then replied, "You make joke?"

"Sorry, it's been a long day."

"They still follow?"

"I doubt it. It would be hard to get tangled up with a moving trawler without causing substantial damage. Besides, they seemed to know our first stop but they would never guess our second."

"Is far, this Mistake?"

"Not far. At this rate we will be there mid-afternoon tomorrow."

Thérèse started into the cabin, "I sleep now. You wake me in two hours. Then you sleep. Okay?"

"Okay."

Thérèse disappeared below. Ben could hear her getting comfortable in the forward cabin. He retrieved his cell phone from the companionway shelf and turned it on. They were about twenty miles offshore but his phone still showed two bars. Enough to try a call. Detective Townsend answered immediately.

"Detective Townsend, here."

"This is Ben Slade. We've been chased by a power boat."

"Where are you?"

"East of Damariscove on the Maine coast."

"We?" asked Townsend.

"What do you mean?"

"You said *we've been chased*."

"More about that in a moment. Who knows that I'm out on my boat?"

"Nobody from my office. Whoever dropped off your car at the marina. Who else did you tell?"

"George Rawlings loaned me his car before I left. Thought it would be safer. I told no one else. Someone could have seen *Emma* leave the marina."

"Is the power boat still in pursuit?"

"I doubt it. They ran into a trawler in the fog. We haven't seen them for a couple of hours."

"Good. Now, who is the *we?*" demanded Townsend.

Ben lowered his voice, "I'm not sure. Did you know that Marie had a twin sister named Thérèse?"

"We just found that out. A Thérèse LaFontaine left a rental car in the marina parking lot. Is Thérèse with you?"

Ben ignored the question, "I need to know something about the body you have."

Townsend was silent.

"Does she have a small tattoo of a butterfly on her abdomen?"

"I'll check the coroner's report, but it's at the office. I'll have to call you tomorrow."

"I'll call you. One more thing. You might be on the lookout for any damaged power boats returning to the harbor. We never actually saw it but it sounded like a big cigarette boat."

"I'm way ahead of you. We'll check on Portland and Bath as well. Now who is with you?" asked Townsend.

"She says she's Thérèse but I'll tell you tomorrow when I'm sure," said Ben as he hung up.

Ben decided to take a four-hour watch instead of two. The solitude would do him good. Wouldn't have been able to sleep anyway, he mumbled to himself. *Emma* moved effortlessly through the darkness. The masthead light cast a pale dim glow over the deck as it was reflected and diffused by the fog. Finally, he awoke Thérèse. He showed her how to turn on and off the radar transmissions. And how to deal with the autopilot.

"Wake me in two hours or sooner if you need me," Ben said as he headed below.

"*Oui, mon capitán,*" came the reply.

Ben smiled and continued below, throwing himself fully clothed into the forward berth. He was out in five seconds.

He awoke at dawn. Thérèse had evidently decided to let him sleep. He checked their position on the GPS. They had made good time during the night. Then he brewed some coffee and brought two cups to the cockpit. Thérèse smiled at the gesture. The fog was just as dense as it had been the night before. Visibility was barely ten yards beyond the bow. The only difference was that, with the sunlight, the fog was now white instead of black.

"Another six hours to Magic Island," he said to break the silence.

"You talk on the phone last night?" she asked.

"Yes, to Detective Townsend of the police."

"You tell him about me?"

"He already knew about you. They found your rental car at the marina."

"Is Townsend a good policeman?"

"What do you mean?"

"Do you trust this man?" she asked. "Last night someone knows where we are."

"Yes, I trust Townsend. He knew I left on the boat, but he didn't know where I would go."

"Who knew? Who did you tell?"

"I didn't tell anyone."

"Then how?"

"Someone who knows me well figured that I would probably stop at Damariscove."

"Would George know where you go?"

Ben was surprised by the question. "George knew I left on the boat and could have figured it out. I've taken him to that island in the past. But he would be the last person I would think to cause me harm. And what motive would he have?"

"The Gerard book," she said.

"I don't believe it. It's just not possible."

Thérèse fell silent and Ben was left with his thoughts as *Emma* pushed on through the fog. Ben couldn't believe that George was involved. And yet, who else knew about the text, about his leaving on *Emma*, and about where his first stop might be? George. And Frieda. He turned it over in his mind. And finally decided that it was impossible that either of the Rawlings could be involved. They just weren't killers.

At three o'clock they passed Great Wass Island, half a mile off their port side although, except for radar, they never had any indication that it was there. Ben got out a trolling rod and trailed a lure behind the boat. He slid the handle of the rod into a holder on the stern. As soon as he turned around there was a strike. *Emma* was moving along at four knots on autopilot. He took the rod out of the holder and handed it to Thérèse who smiled as she found a place on deck where she could play the fish without interference from shrouds or backstay. Ben adjusted the autopilot to take the boat another twenty degrees upwind. Not enough to come about but enough to slow the boat down. Then he looked through the lazerette for the gaff.

Thérèse was having a good time playing the fish. It was a welcome diversion from the stress she had been under for the last twenty four hours.

"*Il est un maquereau,*" she exclaimed when the fish broke the surface. In fifteen minutes it was tired enough to be maneuvered to where Ben could gaff it and pull it onboard. A three-pound mackerel—dinner. Ben killed the fish and got out a bucket so that he could clean it without making a mess of *Emma's* teak decks. Then they returned to their original course. He didn't bother putting the trolling line back in the water.

At five o'clock they approached the inlet that Ben had been aiming for. Where the Damariscove entrance was a horizontal slit on a flat island, this entrance was a vertical slit in a rock cliff between two small islands just off the mainland. The fog was as thick as ever, a sheet of white before them. They could hear the fog horn from the light house on top of the cliff. They could hear the surf breaking on the walls of the cliff. Ben checked the GPS position and adjusted the radar. They were dead on their waypoint and the position of the slit showed bright and clear on the radar. For reasons that Ben never fully understood, the digital charts behind the GPS could be off by enough to cause them problems, but the match of the GPS and the radar were enough for Ben to proceed even though visibility was next to nil. He started the engine, rolled up the genoa, and dropped the main. Giving the helm to Thérèse, he went below to monitor the radar. Watching from on deck wasn't much help. Ben noticed that the ebbing tide was setting them offshore making it difficult to line up the entrance to the west. He called out course corrections to Thérèse.

"Come right five degrees to 285."

"I don't like this."

"Don't worry. We'll be okay. Come right to 285."

"I heard you the first time," she protested.

"How would I know? You're supposed to repeat a course change. Just like in the navy."

A short silence, then she responded, "Right to 2-8-5. Aye, aye, sir."

"Thank you and you don't have to call me *sir*."

The surf pounded louder and louder. Still there was no change in the white sheet before them. Thérèse strained to see ahead, but to no avail. Their approach seemed endless although it probably took less than twenty minutes.

"Come right to 290."

The surf seemed deafening.

"Right to 2-9-0. Etes-vous sûr?"

"Bien sûr, ma chère."

Thérèse mumbled something in French that Ben couldn't quite pick up, but he was sure that it wasn't pleasant. Just when it sounded like the surf was surrounding them, the walls of the cliff appeared on both sides, not ten yards away. They had split the entrance down the middle. Thérèse gave a long sigh and a muffled *merde*. Ben came up to the cockpit and throttled back the engine to its lowest forward speed.

"I'm going forward to direct you to the anchorage," he said. Pointing with his index finger, he said, "This means *look at that*. Usually something to avoid, like a rock." Pointing with his whole hand, palm vertical, he said, "This means *go that direction*. Okay? Don't confuse one with the other."

"Okay. Don't confuse."

Pointing with his whole hand, palm vertical, to the stern, he said, "And this…"

"Oui, oui, this is reverse engine."

"Okay."

"Okay, okay."

Once through the cliff, the inlet opened out gradually into several little bays nestled among adjoining islands. After a brief study of the chart, Ben selected a protected indentation that was supposed to have reasonable holding. Slowly they picked their way through the rocks to the chosen spot. He signaled Thérèse to reverse until they had stopped their forward motion. He dropped the anchor and kept her going in reverse until they had paid out enough chain and had set the anchor. With the islands between them and the open sea, they started picking up a land breeze and the fog showed signs of clearing. Their chosen anchorage was breathtakingly beautiful. They were surrounded by jagged pink and grey granite outcrops with pines stuck into every available crevice. Ben shut down the engine and opened a bottle of Sancerre. They settled in the cockpit.

"I doubt that anyone will find us here," he said.

"Another time I be happy here."

"Yes, this is also a favorite spot of mine but I've never been here with anyone but my father, if that makes you feel more secure."

"Ben, men in cigarette boat are great worry to me."

"I don't think we'll see them again."

"But who know I am with you?"

"Wait, you think they were after you?"

"Of course, after me and the book."

"I see…perhaps you're right. I had just assumed that they were after me because they thought that I had the book."

"Who know I am with you?"

"Nobody knew. If you're right, someone guessed, that's all."

"Who would guess? Who know you were with Marie?"

"Her temporary flat mate. Anybody at the faculty cocktail party—"

"Rawlings?" she asked.

"Yes, of course, Rawlings. But don't worry. We're safe enough here, I would think."

They sat for an hour, wrestling with their thoughts and enjoying the wine. Ben judged that they had about a half an hour of daylight left so he proposed that they prepare dinner. Easier that way. Thérèse put some potatoes on to boil and Ben finished fileting the fish which he dusted with flour and salt. While they were waiting for the potatoes, he found a can of green beans which he heated in a sauce pan. Thérèse set the table in the cabin since the evening air had turned quite cold. When the potatoes were cooked and buttered and the beans were ready, Ben fried the mackerel filets in butter and marjoram in a very hot skillet. Tssst, flip, tssst. Total time less than a minute.

Thérèse seemed amused, "Where you learn this cooking of fish?"

"From an Austrian named Wolfgang. Can't beat it if the fish is very fresh."

"A toast to Austrian Wolfgangs," she said.

Dinner was great, they both agreed. They finished the wine and cleaned up the galley. Ben poured them each a cognac and they bundled up to go back to the cockpit to enjoy the evening. The fog had almost disappeared but the night air was unseasonably cold.

She asked, "The river of warm water in the sea—"

"The Gulf Stream?"

"*Oui*, the Gulf Stream. It does not come here?"

"No, not this far North. It heads off across the Atlantic to keep the Brits from freezing to death."

"Pity."

They watched the stars come out for half an hour.

"We sleep?" she asked.

"Good idea, it's been a long day," said Ben.

Ben had been wondering about sleeping arrangements. The forward cabin was the only reasonable place to sleep unless someone could curl around the settee by the cabin table or slide into the quarter berth which, as usual, was cluttered with equipment. He did have two sleeping bags on board so he didn't think that it would be too much of a problem.

"I fix," she said as she went below.

He sat in the cockpit for another ten minutes. It might be better to give her a little privacy, he thought, while she gets ready for bed. He went below and brushed his teeth in the galley sink.

"Hurry," she said from the forward cabin, "it's cold in here without you."

Ben turned out the light and opened the door to the forward cabin. He could make out, in the half-light, that Thérèse had zipped the sleeping bags together to make a double. She lifted one side to allow Ben to get in. He closed the cabin door, dropped his clothes and jumped in. Normally he slept in the buff, but under the circumstances he retained his briefs.

"*Merde*, it's damp and cold," she said as she wrapped up with him. She was shivering. Ben had one arm underneath her head. With the other, he tucked in the top sleeping bag around them. They lay still, feeling the warmth come back as their collective heat dispelled the cold. It became clear to Ben that Thérèse had gone to bed almost in the buff as well. He was confused, excited, saddened. He didn't know what he was.

"*Bon nuit,*" she whispered.//
"Sleep well," he replied.

When he awoke the next morning Thérèse was already up and dressed. He could hear her rustling in the galley accompanied by a quiet, "*Ce qui est faux?*"

"There's a cutoff switch for the gas next to the stove," he called out as he searched for his clothes. He realized that she had watched him light the burners the night before but she must have missed the first step of the cutoff switch.

"*Merci,*" she said as she finally got the coffee going. "Why this cutoff switch?"

"In America we use propane which requires a cutoff switch to keep any gas leaks out of the boat. In Europe you use butane which is lighter and doesn't pose the same problem."

"Cutoff switch," she repeated.

The morning air was clear and quite cold. Ben searched through the clothes locker and found two base layers and turtlenecks—his and those left behind by Christine. He dressed and took Christine's clothes to Thérèse in the main cabin. She eyed the clothes and asked, "She won't mind?"

"No, she's gone forever. Never liked the cold anyway."

Thérèse pulled off her bulky sweater and put on the base layer and turtleneck, followed by the sweater again. Ben marveled at the way she exposed her body to him as if it were the most natural thing in the world. With a body like hers there would be no reason to be shy, he thought.

"Girlfriend?" she asked.

"Wife. Well…ex-wife."

"Sorry."

Ben cooked some Quaker Oats which he served with milk and brown sugar. Thérèse peered into her bowl. "This is porridge for children, no?"

"It's good for you. It'll stick to your ribs."

"Stick to your ribs," she mumbled as she dug in.

After breakfast Ben got out the spinning rod and tried his luck casting from the foredeck. He kept at it for an hour even though there was not so much as a nibble. Finally, he got out the bosun's chair so that Thérèse could crank him up the mast on the main halyard. He installed the radar reflector on the upper shroud where it would give them better visibility. Throughout the morning they spoke little. There was sandwich material to make a lunch for the two of them but it was becoming clear to Ben that their time was limited. If they didn't make a stop in one of coastal towns to buy some food, they would have to start the trip back. After lunch he decided to see how Thérèse felt about going home.

"It's nice to be safe for a while but we're starting to run out of food."

"But we have to go back soon?"

"I'm afraid so. Perhaps we can help the police find Marie's killer."

"Perhaps, but maybe the killer find us."

After a short silence, Thérèse added, "I catch dinner now."

As before, Ben helped Thérèse launch the dinghy. He went below to the nav station to update the ship's log with their position while she loaded the dinghy with the fishing gear. He came back on deck to see her row out of the anchorage to the north. When she was out of earshot, he dialed Detective Townsend.

"Townsend, here. Where the hell have you been? I thought you were going to call me back."

"Sorry, we've had dense fog and it took us longer than I thought to find a safe refuge."

"Where are you now?"

"Farther down east near Mistake Island."

"You can't keep this disappearing act going forever."

"I realize that. We'll be back soon. What did you find out about the tattoo?"

"The body has a small tattoo of a butterfly on the abdomen. And, to answer your next question, the tattoo is real. It's permanent."

Ben paused for a moment. Townsend allowed him to collect his thoughts.

"Detective Townsend, it's possible that you have the body of Thérèse LaFontaine."

"How do you know that?"

"Because Marie didn't have a tattoo."

"How do you know *that*?"

"Because we...got intimate the evening before she was killed."

Detective Townsend did his best to curb his anger. "When were you planning to tell me that?"

"I wasn't. Didn't think that you needed to know. I didn't kill her."

"So you say, but you're not helping me find out who did. In fact, you're clearly obstructing justice. And a fugitive from the crime investigation. And withholding—"

"It's possible that Marie, with a fake tattoo, has been here with me on the boat, pretending to be Thérèse. She's frightened out of her mind that the killers are still looking for her."

Townsend was quiet for a good twenty seconds. His mind ran through the new possibilities. The case was spinning out of control and he didn't like it. After Ben had allowed his bombshell to sink in, he added, "And I'm pretty sure that the motive had to do with the research she was doing on a French text with George Rawlings."

Townsend was ready to explode. The logical, professional part of his brain kept reminding him that he needed to keep reasonable relations with Ben until he found out everything he needed to know. He could always throw him in jail later.

"We'll identify the body for sure. And we'll talk again with Professor Rawlings. But you...you get your ass back here. And bring whoever you have there with you."

"Yes, sir. We'll be back in a couple of days. Against the prevailing wind, you know. And if you don't hear from me, it's because my cell phone is dying. Didn't bring the charger."

The afternoon before, *Emma* had entered the passage between the cluster of islands from the east after they had cleared the rest of Mistake Island. Now the stowaway rowed north between two of the islands, toward the mainland. At first she rowed slowly leaning over the side from time to time to check the bottom as if she were looking for a good spot to fish. She had no idea if Ben was watching and she didn't want to raise his suspicions. But once past the islands she rowed vigorously north and west. Before she boarded the dinghy she had taken the opportunity to scan Ben's chart to learn that a town on the mainland was only three miles away.

The inflatable dinghy rowed like a slug. After an hour and a half, she could see the outskirts of the town. She found a dock in front of a small house that seemed like a good place to leave the dinghy. She knew that, sooner or later, Ben would realize that she wasn't coming back and that he would come looking for her. If she could leave the dinghy here, he could see it and would be able to retrieve it. The water looked deep enough for *Emma*.

As she approached the dock a tall, elderly gentleman in a plaid wool shirt appeared from the house, "It's a private dock, miss."

"Oh, yes, thank you. We have something of an emergency. My husband is still with our boat. I came in by dinghy to find some help. Please, would you mind if I left the dinghy here while we get things sorted out?"

"Well, guess not in that case."

"Oh thank you, sir. You are so kind," she said placing her hand lightly on the man's shoulder. She tied up the dinghy at the end of the dock.

"Better leave lots of painter," he said. "Tide's going out."

"Yes, I understand," she said retying the dinghy.

"Not to worry, ma'am. I'll keep an eye on'er."

"Oh thank you again," she said as she gathered her backpack. "One of us will be back soon to pick up the dinghy. Is there a taxi in town?"

"Yep, just the one."

She walked quickly off the dock and headed for town. Turning toward the man she waved. "Thank you, thank you." And she was gone.

Ben busied himself with putting *Emma* back in order after their long night's sail. After two hours, he began to wonder what had happened to Thérèse. He wondered if she was having more trouble than usual finding a fish. He went to the food locker under the berth in the forward cabin to see what he might have to go with a fish dinner. He noticed that Thérèse's backpack was missing. In its place he found a note.

Can't go back with you.
Hope the police don't cause
you too much trouble.
Please be careful. Sorry.
      Thérèse

"Damn it," was all that Ben could say. He checked his watch. He would have about two more hours of daylight. Maybe he could catch up with her. Weighing anchor, he motored carefully through the rocks out of the anchorage in the direction she had taken with the dinghy. Soon he found himself in Moosabec Reach which separates the islands from the mainland. There he had to make a choice, right or left. The coast was typical Maine wilderness with majestic rocks and trees, completely devoid of human evidence. He chose left as Indian River, the nearest town, was only three miles up the coast to the northwest. He kept scanning the shore for his dinghy.

Half an hour later he got lucky. There, on an old private dock on the southern edge of town, was his dinghy. He had no idea if the dock had deep water but he didn't feel that he had much choice. Carefully monitoring the depth sounder, he slowly approached the end of the dock and tied up alongside. The elderly gentleman again appeared from the house.

"Suppose you know that this is a private dock," he said.

"Sorry, sir. Just here to collect my dinghy."

"Yep. Your wife said you might be by."

"Did you happen to see where she went?"

"Yep."

Ben waited for the rest of the answer. He had forgotten that he was in Maine. Finally he gave up.

"Where did she go?"

"Don't rightly know. She grabbed a cab, the only one in town, and she left. Said that you had some kind of emergency."

"The only emergency I have right now is catching up with her."

"Well, she seemed in a big hurry. Women."

Ben realized that further pursuit was futile. A west wind was freshening and his berth on the dock was soon to be untenable, even if he was permitted to stay, which seemed unlikely. Without a word, the gentleman helped him load the dinghy onto *Emma's* foredeck. Ben thanked him and cast off. He needed a good night's sleep before heading home so he decided to return to his original anchorage. It started to get dark before he arrived, but the track left in the GPS from the outbound trip lead him through the rocks to the spot he had just left. He set the hook in the dark and turned on the anchor light.

Dinner was a steaming bowl of Dinty Moore's Stew. Hearty fare, or so it said on the can. In reality, a stringent test for the proposition that everything tastes great at sea. A bottle of Cabernet Sauvignon helped make the stew almost palatable. He was reminded of the famous quote, "I like cooking with wine, sometimes I even add it to the food." Ben put on a Bruch violin concerto and sat in the cockpit, sipping the wine.

Depression set in. He missed Marie or Thérèse or whoever the hell she was. Even with all the stress of the past few days, she was good to have around. He was sorry that he had shared his thoughts on her identity with Townsend. But maybe that would help unravel the mystery. But it also might put Marie in more danger. If, indeed, she *was* Marie. He would help her if he could. But what could he do? He could take the text back to Townsend and help the police follow any leads that it might offer. His mental ramblings stopped with a jolt. The text. He went below and checked the bookshelf over the settee where he had placed the text. It was gone. Shit. Did she still need the text? Or did she not want anyone else to have it? Shit. He checked his wallet which he kept on the companionway shelf and found it devoid of cash except for ten dollars. Another reason to head home. He felt used, confused, and alone. He turned off the music and fell asleep alone in the forward cabin.

Return

Ben had the anchor up at first light. The previous season he had installed a remote switch for the anchor windlass so that he could raise the anchor from the steering station. It was useful when sailing alone in that he could position the boat and control the windlass at the same time. It worked perfectly and gave him some small comfort that he was on top of things.

The morning mist didn't look like the Maine fog that could be around all day long and the west wind had moderated to twelve knots. His intention was to head west along the coast, stopping at anchor when he got too tired. Mt. Desert was to be avoided. Too many tourists, even early in the season. A full day of beating, sometimes motor sailing, got him as far as Isle au Haut where he anchored in a little cove just before sunset. His thoughts had never left Marie and the events of the past few days. He still was not completely sure if his stowaway had been Marie or Thérèse, but he seemed to remember that her English had improved when they were being chased out of Damariscove by the cigarette boat. The scales were tipping in favor of Marie. But maybe he would never know for sure. Whoever she was, by this time she was probably on a plane to France. In all likelihood he would never see her again. It bothered him that he seemed to be depressed by the prospect.

The next morning he was up at dawn. He made a large thermos of coffee and tried to raise the anchor. It wouldn't budge. He remembered when he checked the chart on the anchorage that the bottom was considered to be questionable—some weed, some rock, some sand. However when he set the anchor, it seemed to dig in and hold just fine. He preferred the CQR plow anchor that usually held well in all conditions. Now his CQR was stuck under something that wasn't about to move. He went forward to maneuver the windlass directly. Down and up, down and up. Nothing doing. He left some slack in the chain and returned to the helm to move the boat in various directions. Still stuck solid. *Emma* was anchored in only twenty feet of water so it would be possible for Ben to dive down to see what was the matter. However he figured that the water temperature this early in the season would probably give him a heart attack before he got to the bottom. What's next, he thought. *Ah, the gypsy. Now where the hell is it?* He searched both lazarettes and found his gypsy, a four-foot length of chain with a shackle. He picked up one of the fifty-foot lines that he used to pass though locks and went forward. Leaning over the bow he looped the gypsy around the anchor chain and shackled it to itself and to the line. Then he tightened the anchor chain and lowered the gypsy to the bottom. The idea was to position the gypsy down the shank of the anchor near its head. Then he let out some of the gypsy's line and secured it to a cleat. He returned to the helm and let out the anchor chain as he motored forward. It worked. The gypsy pulled the anchor out from underneath the offending rock. Ben retrieved everything and was set to go.

The second day of his passage home brought a brisk west wind of over twenty knots. Progress was difficult indeed. This is why they call it *down east*, he thought. *Emma* did her best to weather but the building waves made progress slow and painful. Every so often a wave would catch the bow and bring *Emma* almost to a stop with a back-wrenching jolt accompanied by spray that covered the cutter from stem to stern. With each jolt, Ben instinctively lowered his head to keep the spray out of his foul weather gear. He silently urged *Emma* forward as if she were a tired race horse.

The strain was taking its toll on him. He hadn't fully recovered from the all-night sail on the trip down east. Now he was being pushed to his limits. *You have no idea as to where your limits are.* The voice of his high school track coach, Coach Copeland. Copeland had a logical argument to support his premise on limits. Suppose you're running wind sprints, a diabolical training exercise in which you sprint the straight part of the track and walk the ends, over and over again. Suppose you're beat and your body feels like it can't run another step, you've hit your limit. Then suppose you, through sheer willpower, force yourself to sprint one more hundred yard stretch. See, you didn't know what your limit was. And you still don't because you might just be able to force yourself to do just one more sprint. Ben had to smile at the memory. He liked the coach's proof; it used the same logic that some mathematical proofs use in proving the properties of different types of infinite series. Then Ben laughed as another Coach Copeland memory surfaced. The coach had always told them not to smoke or stay out late. However, the best long-distance runner on the team was Pete, a tough kid from the wrong side of the tracks who smoked and hung out at the local pool hall. Ben, with two of his team mates, confronted the coach with this inconsistency, "But what about Pete? He's a great runner and he doesn't follow the rules." Coach Copeland didn't miss a beat. "Just think of what he might have been," was his patent answer. Ben reasoned later that Pete won races simply because he wouldn't allow himself to be beaten.

Late in the afternoon he anchored off of Monhegan Island. He was exhausted. For all of their efforts, the day's run only amounted to thirty miles in the direction of home. During the day the conditions had been rough enough that the autopilot functioned only marginally. As a result Ben had managed to have only a quick ham and cheese sandwich and a bottle of beer. Now at anchor in the relative calm of the lee of the island he realized how hungry he was. Tired and hungry. Most of his body was telling him to lie down and sleep. His stomach was shouting something else. He searched the fridge and the food locker for something to eat. Feeding his stowaway on the trip down east had done a good job of depleting his stores. He couldn't face another dinner of Dinty Moore's Stew although there was still one can left in the locker. Finally he put on a pot of water for spaghetti and opened a jar of Newman's Own Sockarooni pasta sauce. He opened a bottle of Pinot Noir and had a glass while he was waiting for the pot to boil. The next thing he knew the hissing of the boiling water hitting the burner below woke him up. He added the pasta to the pot and managed to stay awake while it cooked. He strained it and added the sauce cold on top. Not the dinner he was used to cooking for himself but better than nothing. Ah, the joys of solo sailing, he thought as he fell asleep again.

The following day the wind gods smiled upon *Emma* and Ben. The westerlies veered to the northwest at a constant fifteen knots. A vigorous close reach, just the kind of conditions that *Emma* reveled in. He altered his course to sail a little closer to land to give the seas less room to build up. The autopilot worked fine giving him a chance to rest and enjoy the trip. Well, perhaps enjoying the trip was something of an over statement. What the improved conditions did do, however, was to allow Ben to think about his situation. He was floored by the extent of what he didn't know. Who sent the cigarette boat to look for them? How did they know where to look? Did they have orders to kill or just to retrieve the text? Who was his stowaway, Marie or Thérèse? Was Bonsans involved? Were the Rawlings involved? Who was the temporary flat mate? And what role did he play? Ben had only questions, no answers.

Emma pulled into her home marina at eight o'clock that evening. Ben tied up, took a shower, had a glass of Cognac, and fell asleep. His last waking thoughts were that he would have to deal with food, and Detective Townsend, in the morning.

His morning activities didn't come in that order. At seven o'clock he was startled by a rap on the hull and a crisp, "Permission to come aboard." Townsend didn't wait for a reply and met Ben in the cockpit as he was struggling to pull on some clothes on his way up the companionway.

"Good morning, Detective Townsend."

"Saw that you were back. Thought it would be best to get some things settled as soon as possible."

"Agreed, but first I need some coffee and some breakfast."

"When did you come in?" And then, after a pause, "Is she with you?"

"She's not here and I need some coffee and some breakfast."

Ben picked up sunglasses, the boat key, and his wallet from the companionway shelf. He locked up *Emma* and headed toward the waterfront diner next to the marina. Townsend reluctantly followed.

"She, whoever she was, took the dinghy and jumped ship three days ago at Indian River east of Mt. Desert. I tried to catch up with her but failed. I've no idea where she went. I managed to retrieve my dinghy and sailed back here. Arrived last night."

They settled in a booth in the near-deserted diner. The waitress, a perky thirty-something townie with short red hair, brought coffee first and took the order second.

"Hi, Ben. Haven't seen you since last season," she said.

"Hello, Evie, how have you been?"

"Good, good. Missed you. Full breakfast as usual?"

"Yes, thanks. How's Skip?"

"Nothing but coffee for me," interjected Townsend. The pleasantries were beginning to infuriate him. He had a murder case on his hands, for Christ's sake, and his star witness was chatting up a waitress.

Evie stopped short, annoyed at Townsend's manner. Living in a small university town meant, of course, that she knew who Townsend was. His inflated view of his own importance was common knowledge in the community. "Skip's just fine," she said in defiance. "I'll tell him you said hello. I'll be right back with your breakfast."

When they were alone, Townsend went to work.

"Tell me everything you know about the Gerard text."

"Did you talk to Rawlings?"

"Yes, he seemed a bit surprised that you suggested that I go back to him."

Ben was perplexed. "He shouldn't have been. He suggested the text as a possible motive to me in the first place."

"Strange. Perhaps he's changed his mind," said Townsend, making a mental note to reopen the discussion with Rawlings in the future. He hated inconsistencies and loose ends. Either Rawlings or Slade were not being forthright. Hiding something. He could smell it.

"So tell me what you know about the text," Townsend repeated.

"Only what I told you before. That Marie thought that she had deciphered from the text where the treasure was hidden. That I helped her correct her findings and that she was ecstatic. Rawlings, himself, told me that he thought that Marie's discovery might have been the reason for her murder."

"And you have the text?"

Ben shook his head. "*Had* the text. It disappeared with my stowaway."

"Jesus Christ," said Townsend. "I should throw you in jail just to keep you from mucking up the investigation any further. Do you realize how much confusion you've caused in this thing? Did you look at the text?"

"Yes, but I couldn't confirm her conclusions. Only to point out where she had made a bad assumption."

"Why couldn't you confirm her conclusions?"

"French baroque poetry isn't my thing. I'm a mathematician, remember? I could only help her with a problem in triangulation and longitude."

"Then you don't know where the supposed treasure is hidden?"

"Haven't a clue."

Evie returned to drop Ben's breakfast in front of him. She had overheard only "…supposed treasure is hidden" but that was enough for her throw a barb at the detective.

"If you find the treasure, I hope you will share it with me," she said as she turned on her heel and left.

Townsend was so disturbed that he practically left his seat, but he managed to gain control and only glared at the waitress as she retreated to the kitchen. Townsend resumed his questioning.

"How do you know about the tattoo on your…stowaway? Did you sleep with her too?"

Ben really wanted to help with the investigation but Townsend's attitude was making it difficult to cooperate in good faith.

"No, I didn't have sex with her. But she practically showed me the tattoo when she was taking a sponge bath."

"Why would she do that?" asked Townsend.

"To make me think that she was Thérèse, of course."

"Then you think that she *was* Marie?"

Ben returned to his breakfast shaking his head, "I don't know. I really don't know. I know that she was one step ahead of me the whole time."

"Professors," said Townsend under his breath. "God blessed me with a professor as my star witness."

Ben continued to devour his breakfast. He couldn't believe how hungry he was.

"Was your stowaway identical to Marie?" Townsend asked.

"Yes, they were identical twins. Thérèse's hair was a bit shorter and a shade darker. Otherwise, except for the tattoo, exactly the same."

"You said that she got away in your dinghy. You weren't at a dock."

"No, we were anchored among some little islands off the coast."

"And you just let her go off in the dinghy?"

"We were running low on food, I didn't know I would have to feed two people, and she was very good at catching fish. She had caught dinner before at Damariscove. I never suspected that she would take off."

"So when she didn't come back, you went looking?"

"Right. Indian River was about three miles away, so I motored that direction until I saw the dinghy tied up to a dock."

"And she was gone."

"Yes, the man who owned the dock said that she took a taxi."

"And you have no idea where she went?"

"No, the town does have a small airport and a bus terminal. She could be anywhere."

"You don't think that she came back here?"

"That's certainly a possibility."

"Why wouldn't she have come back with you?"

"I was trying to convince her to contact you and she didn't want to deal with the police. She said that she wanted to deal with this in her own way."

"Then she probably got back here before you did."

Ben realized that, if he hadn't been so hungry, Townsend might have ruined his breakfast.

Ben looked at the bill and felt his wallet. Luckily, the diner was cheap so that his remaining ten dollars and change covered it. He paid Evie at the register. Townsend insisted on paying for his own coffee, "Official business, you know. It wouldn't do to be treating an investigating police officer on duty."

Ben and Evie ignored his comments.

Returning Ben's change, Evie said, "Skip asks about you often. He had such a wonderful time that day."

Ben smiled, "Yes, so did I. We were flying that afternoon. If that didn't scare him off sailing, you have a life-long sailor on your hands."

"Well, Ben, anytime you need crew, we're available," said Evie with a short curtsey.

Outside the diner Townsend asked, "So who's Skip?"

"Evie's ten year old son. Last summer I noticed that he was often hanging around the boats. I was going out for an afternoon sail so I asked him to ask his parents if he could go along. He said that he only had one. Then he ran off to the diner and returned with Evie who announced that she was coming along. It was a nice afternoon."

"Right, she really looked like she was interested in sailing. Do you hit on everything in a skirt?"

Ben stopped and grabbed Townsend by his arm. Townsend bristled but didn't resist.

"Look, I want to help you solve this murder, but you've got to lay off the womanizing comments," Ben said with some force.

"Sorry. Didn't realize that it was a sensitive issue."

"It's not an issue. Just lay off."

"Sorry."

Ben was surprised at his own actions. Emotional, physical reactions were unusual for him. He released his grip and continued walking back to the boat. Then he stopped and grabbed Townsend's arm again. The detective was about to react when he saw Ben's face. Ben was staring at a figure on the dock looking down at *Emma*.

"That's him," Ben said. "That's the temporary flat mate I told you about."

Townsend glanced at the figure and led Ben behind a panel truck, out of the line of sight from the dock. Ben started to protest, but Townsend stopped him.

"Let us take care of this," he said as he called the station for some help. He asked for an officer in plain clothes and an unmarked car to join him at the marina. He asked for a patrol car to go to Ben's home to check things out before Ben arrived. Townsend watched the dark young man for a few minutes.

"He seems to be alone," said Townsend.

"You're not going to apprehend him?" asked Ben.

"There's time for that. Let's first find out where he leads us. If he's looking for you, he may be important in this thing."

"But what—"

"Can you get to your car without being seen?" asked the detective.

"Yes, I think so."

"Then, I'd like you to go home. Park on the next street and enter by the back door. Just stay out of sight for a while. We'll take care of our temporary flat mate here. I have a few questions I'd like to ask him."

While Ben was considering how to get to his car unseen, the young man walked back to a motorbike in the parking lot and started to leave. Townsend was instantly on his phone trying to connect his arriving plain clothes help with the departing suspect. He evidently was successful as Ben saw an arriving car turn around and follow the motorbike. Townsend moved quickly to his car and called to Ben over his shoulder, "Go home. Charge your cell phone. I'll call you."

Ben collected his gear from the boat and drove home as ordered. Entering the house by the back door, he unlocked the front door for the middle-aged uniformed policeman waiting on the front porch.

"Detective Townsend wanted me to check things out. Okay with you?" he said.

"Absolutely fine by me. Look anywhere you like. Under the bed. Anywhere."

"Can't be too careful," the officer said. "Don't have too many murders around here."

"Have we ever had one?"

"No, can't say that we have."

The officer started on his tour of the house while Ben plugged in his cell phone and sat at his desk with a beer. His list of unread emails was especially long. His graduate assistant needed to talk to him urgently about the multiple choice final exam. Urgently. Ben smiled. There were some emails from a few of the students strongly protesting the underhanded, unfair form of the test. There was an email from the head of the department requesting that Ben contact him 'when it was convenient.' Ben was still smiling. With the events of the past week, he had completely forgotten about the exam, but he was more than ready to defend his position. Students complain about exams, no matter what. He might as well give them something to complain about.

There was another email from an address he didn't recognize. It simply said, "Please call 307 583 5321."

It looked like a cell phone number, but it wasn't one that Ben recognized.

"Why the mystery?" he mumbled to himself. He dialed the number from his desk phone. After several rings he reached a voice mail message. A woman's voice, in French. He tried to convince himself that the voice was Thérèse's or Marie's, but he had to admit that he couldn't tell for sure. He left a message that he had called.

The uniformed officer completed his tour of the house and let himself out the front door. He assured Ben that he would be coming by periodically to check things out. Ben locked the front door after he left and busied himself with answering some routine emails. He called his graduate assistant.

"Sid, sorry to leave you in the lurch. Sounds like the multiple choice exam has had some impact."

"You can say that again, Professor. I was afraid that they were going to tar and feather me."

"That bad, huh. How did they do?"

Sid laughed. "Quite a wide distribution. A median of 68 which you have to say is not too great on a final."

"Yes, I thought that we taught them more than that."

Sid laughed again, "But the distribution was bimodal. A number of them figured it out, took great care, and did well. A bunch of them *thought* that they figured it out, raced through it, and bombed."

"Yes, but it was easy to grade, right?"

"Right, but in the future, I think that I would rather struggle with four problems and partial credit."

"So the final grades are all in?"

"All done. It's been a pleasure working for you."

"Thanks, Sid, it's been a pleasure working with you, too. Good luck on your orals."

"Thanks, Professor, I'll need it."

"Who else is on your committee?"

"Professors Irslinger and Crowley, and yourself, of course."

"Irslinger likes to stir things up a bit, likes to see if he can catch a candidate off guard."

"So I've heard."

Ben paused. He had another reason to be concerned about Irslinger. Sid was probably gay although in the three years that Ben had been his dissertation advisor, the subject had never come up. Irslinger was openly critical of gays stating once in a faculty meeting, "God never meant for anyone to live that way." The faculty meeting had gone silent. No one agreed with him, but no one was willing to take on the aging, combative professor. Ben felt that Sid's dissertation was strong and that his general grasp of related mathematical fields was sound. He didn't want to see Sid run into difficulties for reasons unrelated to his mathematics.

"Take a look at Cantor's paradox," Ben said.

"Cantor's paradox?" exclaimed Sid, "What does that have to do with—"

"Yes, orals are supposed to be about your research topic but in practice the examiners feel that they have the latitude to probe related areas."

"Cantor's paradox has absolutely nothing to do with—"

"Right," said Ben, "but it's one of Irslinger's favorite questions so that he can lead you into the Burali-Forti paradox."

"Jesus," murmured Sid, "but why are you telling me this?"

"Just trying to level the playing field."

"Irslinger will give me trouble because I'm gay?"

"I'm afraid so. But don't be too concerned, you'll do fine. Just remember to sit on your hands."

"What? Sit on my hands?"

Ben laughed, almost sorry he had started this last line of thought. "When I was a young man seriously playing in chess tournaments, an old man, who had just thrashed me in a quick game asked me if I would mind if he gave me a piece of advice that would improve my game one hundred percent. Under the circumstances, I couldn't refuse. He said, *Sit on your hands.* And he left. I was offended and confused, but I later surmised that he meant that the extra two seconds that it would take me to extricate my hand before I made a move would give me a chance to think it over. I never actually sat on my hands during a match but the idea helped improve my game."

"So I should *sit on my hands* during the orals?"

"Metaphorically. It's good to look like you know the answer, but you can take your time to formulate your response."

"Thanks, Professor, I understand."

"Not to worry, you'll do just fine. See you next week."

Ben reclined on the couch and stared at the cell phone number that he had copied from the email message. The French voice mail almost had to be related to Thérèse or Marie or her murder. His cell phone hadn't been working the last couple of days so it wouldn't have been possible for anyone to contact him. Could it have been Thérèse? His pondering finished when he fell asleep.

He awoke to a knock at the door. It was still light outside, but he could tell that the sun was on its way down. He must have slept through the afternoon. It crossed his mind that he may be getting too old for this overnight, solo sailing business. Nonsense, he just needed to catch up on his sleep. He stumbled to the front door but nobody was there. The knocking resumed. It was coming from the back door. He made his way to the back door, smoothed down his hair with his hand, and ushered in Detective Townsend carrying a take-out pizza.

Townsend smiled and said, "Looks like you've had a chance to rest. Thought you might like some dinner. Pepperoni and mushrooms okay?"

Ben was still struggling to wake up from what must have been a very deep sleep. In fact he felt that he still must be dreaming. Here was Townsend, a smiling Townsend no less, bringing him dinner and acting like a normal human being.

"Pepperoni and mushrooms sounds perfect."

On their way through the living room, Townsend paused to look at a position set up on the chess board on the coffee table.

"Who's move?" he asked.

"Black."

"You playing a remote game with someone?"

"No, it's a position from a pivotal Alekhine/Capablanca game in the St. Petersburg Tournament in 1914."

"Then why...?" said Townsend, not taking his eyes off the board.

"It's a famous combination. When I can't find an opponent and get bored, I sometimes study the masters."

"Looks like black has a win in six moves with this," said the detective as he moved the black queen to C4.

Ben laughed. "True, but that wasn't discovered until after the tournament. What he, Capablanca, did was to—"

"Right," interrupted Townsend, "the knight sacrifice taking the pawn next to the white king. I didn't see it at first. The king has to move from the back row to take it. Things fall apart for white after that. Mate in about the same number of moves."

Townsend was obviously pleased with himself. Ben would have been annoyed had he not been so impressed by Townsend's ability.

"We'll have to play sometime," said Ben quietly.

"When this is all over," returned the detective.

They sat at the kitchen table while Ben opened a bottle of Merlot. He offered a glass to Townsend.

"Would you like a glass or are you still on duty?"

"A glass would be fine and I'm always on duty, but we've accomplished a great deal today."

"Did you manage to follow the young man on the motor bike?"

"We did indeed. He was quite cautious and tried to make sure that he couldn't be followed. However, he had no reason to expect that he *was* being followed and there were two unmarked cars on our side of the equation, as you people say. We played him off until he led us to his destination."

"Which was where?" Ben stopped eating pizza and looked at Townsend.

"Professor Rawlings' house," said Townsend, eying Ben for his reaction.

Ben put down his piece of pizza. Rawlings. Why would the young man check out *Emma* and then go to Rawlings? Of course, there could have been a number of innocent reasons. Of course.

"What's your take on his connection to Rawlings?" asked Detective Townsend.

"Didn't know that there *was* one. Perhaps he was just trying to find out what happened to Marie. Perhaps the same reason why he was at the marina looking for me. He would have known that she worked with Rawlings and that she was with me before she died. I don't know. What did Rawlings say? I assume that you talked to him."

"We did. At first, he was uncooperative. Said that he had never seen the young man before."

"Why did he say the young man came to his house?"

Townsend smiled, "You'll make a detective, yet. He made up some story about the young man asking about Thérèse."

"Made up?"

"Yes, made up. He was lying. Don't know why, yet. But he was lying."

"How can you tell he was lying?"

"Been in this business a long time. I can just tell. That's why you didn't end up in jail on day one. I knew that you weren't telling us everything, but what you told us was basically the truth."

Ben thought for a minute while he returned to his slice of pizza.

"What did Frieda, Mrs. Rawlings, say about it?" asked Ben.

"She wasn't there. Business trip to Europe, according to her husband."

"And the young man?"

"We picked him up when he left Rawlings. Currently a guest at our local lockup. He's Hakim Taflon, an Algerian national of French descent. Been in this country on a student visa, but hasn't really attended any classes, as far as we can tell. We're still working on what he's been doing during the six months he's been here. Interpol says that he's clean but his brother is connected to a crime organization involved in drug smuggling in the south of France."

"What was his connection to Marie?" asked Ben.

"Other than being her *temporary flat mate*? Don't know that either. Now *he* is *really* uncooperative. Seems to be expecting us to bring out the rubber hoses and do a number on him. Too bad we can't. Might get to the bottom of this quicker."

"Right, and he might be an innocent bystander in all of this."

Townsend laughed. "No, whatever he is, he's not innocent. I'd bet my pension on it."

"But without more evidence, sooner or later you'll have to let him go, right?"

"Maybe later than sooner. It seems that he's been spending his time in Boston around BU although he failed to register for classes. The police there are trying to turn up any connection that might enable us to hold him a bit longer. Who knows, he might even be guilty of something." Townsend chuckled.

Ben poured more wine and they ate in silence. Ben had too much to think about. Taflon to Rawlings' house. Frieda to Europe. The email message to call a cell phone belonging to a French-speaking person. And then there was Detective Townsend. He was obviously pleased that he was finally making some headway in the case, but for Townsend, he seemed almost buoyant; well, at least, almost human. The fact that Townsend was sharing so much information on the case indicated that he considered Ben a partner of sorts in solving the mystery. As with those people accustomed to sharing secrets, Ben felt obligated to tell the detective about the email, but he hesitated. What if it was Thérèse and she needed Ben's help? On the other hand, if she was in danger, perhaps she would be better off in police custody.

When they had finished the pizza, Ben went to his computer and printed off the email message which he handed to Townsend.

"I tried to call this number and got a voice message in French. I have no idea who it might be or even if it's relevant, but I thought you'd like to know."

The detective read the email and turned to Ben, "Thank you. You should continue to try to make contact and let us know. We'll find out who it belongs to but won't take any action until we talk to you."

Townsend got up and walked to the back door. He folded up the copy of the email and held it up before putting it into his coat pocket.

"Thank you," he said again and left by the back door.

"Thanks for dinner," Ben called after him.

Ben tried the email phone number again but got the same result. Then he dialed George Rawlings who answered on the third ring.

"George, this is Ben. Got back last night. I'd like to come over for a drink and talk over a few things."

"Did you know that the police were here asking more questions?"

"Yes, I did know. Detective Townsend and I just had dinner together."

"Jesus, I think that they suspect that I had something to do with Marie's murder."

"Don't get too worked up. They suspect everybody at the moment. I'll be over in a few minutes. You make the martinis."

Ben was amazed at George's appearance as he entered the Rawlings house. Uncombed hair, clothes that must have been slept in, and bloodshot eyes completed the picture. Frieda always made sure that George was presentable. But with her in Europe and with George under stress, George was going downhill fast. He handed Ben a martini.

"It's bad enough having Marie murdered without being in the police crosshairs as a suspect," he said on their way into the study.

"Well, they know that the Algerian, Hakim, was with Marie the day she died and might be involved in some way. Townsend and I saw him this morning checking out my boat and the police followed him to your house. That's part of why they are suspicious."

"Part? What else?"

"Why did he come here?" asked Ben.

George paused, "He was asking about Thérèse."

"Well, the police aren't buying that part. Probably shouldn't tell you this, but Townsend thinks that you're hiding something."

George sat behind his desk and stared out the window.

"That's all they're going to get out of me at the moment," he said in a low voice.

Ben was surprised by George's response. Townsend's intuition about George must have been right.

"*Do* you have a connection with him?" asked Ben.

George jerked around and faced Ben, "What is this, the Spanish Inquisition? Whose side are you on, anyway?"

"Easy there, big fellow. I'm on the side of truth and justice," said Ben, trying to lighten the mood, "which, I assume, is *your* side. And if the police have a prime suspect, it's me not you."

George visibly deflated and returned his gaze out the window.

"I still can't believe that she's dead," George said slumping down in his chair.

They sat for awhile, nursing their drinks.

Ben broke the silence, "Marie's sister, Thérèse, was a stowaway on *Emma* when I left for Maine."

"What? How in the hell…"

"A long story, but she was there, frightened out of her wits that whoever killed her sister was also after her."

"Are you sure that she was Thérèse and not Marie?"

Ben was startled by the question. He had almost convinced himself that his stowaway had been Thérèse, not Marie. Now he pondered why George would have suspected the switch. He was beginning to have doubts again.

"I'm not really sure," said Ben, "Thérèse, I think."

"Where is she now?" asked George.

"Don't know. She jumped ship in Maine and disappeared. Could be back in France by now as far as I know."

"And the Gerard text," said George, "I assume that she took it with her."

The Spanish Inquisition, my ass, thought Ben. George is deep into this. Knows more about what is going on than any of us.

"Yes, she took the text," said Ben.

Ben finished his drink, made his apologies, and left. He wasn't much for conversation when he had something on his mind and George had given him much to think about. Ben couldn't believe that George would be involved in murder but it was clear that George was involved in something and Ben had to support

Townsend's suspicion that George was hiding the truth. The fact that George seemed to be unraveling didn't help.

On his way home, Ben stopped at the Kung Fu Center for Martial Arts, a two-room operation in a local strip mall run by Master Feeman Ma. Ma was an energetic Chinese immigrant who believed in kindness, hard work, and an iron fist. He was probably in his mid-fifties although it was impossible to tell for sure. Most of Ma's students were pre-teens and teenagers, but he taught some classes for more mature students, as he called them, and he gave private tuition to more advanced students in weapons training. Ben fell into this last category. His specialty was the bo, or six-foot pole.

Ben slipped off his shoes and stood against the wall just inside the door. Master Ma was just finishing his session with some leaping kicks. Ma faced the students and did the kicks with them, rising above them as if he were on wires. Everyone in the class looked ready for the showers. Ben smiled. Ma liked to make sure that his students got their money's worth. Ma made a couple of announcements, dismissed the class, and bowed. They bowed back.

Ma walked over to Ben. Ben bowed and began to apologize for missing a class while he was out on *Emma*, but Ma held up his hand to stop him.

"I hear about murder and you and police. I understand you no come."

"Thank you, Master Ma."

"They find killer?"

"Not yet."

"Victim your girl friend?"

"No, I just met her before she was killed, but she was special to me."

"Very sorry."

"Thank you."

Ma looked down at his feet for a moment before starting again.

"You know, we have tournament in one week. I would like you to give Kung Fu pole demonstration. No competition, just demonstration."

Ben looked at his feet. He loved martial arts and used to do well in general open hand competitions. But now, feeling older and slower, he concentrated on the pole. He knew that he was good, but felt self-conscious in demonstrations.

"I will demonstrate with you. We do *kata*, then mock combat," said Ma with a smile.

Ben smiled and bowed his head. Ma was hard to refuse. He knew that there would be only two, maybe three, people in the audience who would know enough about the art of the pole to appreciate what they were seeing or to judge the correctness of his form. *Kata*s were fine, he knew them backwards and forwards. Doing a combat demonstration with Ma was another story. Ma seemed to enjoy these sessions immensely. An onlooker would hardly be able to follow the blur of poles punctuated by the clash of parry, thrust, and block. For Ben, however, it always turned out to be a subtle lesson, understood, perhaps, only by teacher and student. A tap on the ankle for a foot left too far forward. A light jab in the shoulder for a sweep block that was a bit too slow. Even if the public didn't understand what was happening, Ben knew he was being corrected. And in front of a couple hundred people.

"Okay," said Ben, "I'll do it. When do I have to be there?"

"Next Saturday. University gym. Demonstration during intermission at nine o'clock."

"Fine. Class this Wednesday at the usual time?"

"Right."

Ben bowed and left the center. He took the opportunity to stop at an ATM to replenish his cash supply and drove home, parking in back as before although he doubted that he was still a target. He poured himself a small cognac and headed for the bedroom and a shower. It seemed that he had put in a long day.

Renaissance

"Don't turn on the light, please." A woman's voice stopped him as he reached for the bedroom light switch.

"Marie?" asked Ben in a whisper.

"Of course, it's Marie. Who else would it be? A little hair trim, some hair coloring, a magic marker tattoo and you can't recognize your lover?"

Ben was speechless. He could make out a form sitting at the head of the bed and he walked over to sit at the foot opposite. After a minute all he could say was, "Why?"

"First I needed to hide from the killers and I needed time to sort some things out without the police looking for me."

"But you didn't have to fool me. You could have trusted me."

Marie moved across the bed to be beside Ben. She placed her hand on his knee.

"I'm sorry for that, but if you were convinced that I was Thérèse, then your story to the police would be more, how do you say, credible."

"I would have lied for you. As it was, I told them that I wasn't sure if you were Marie or Thérèse."

"Really? Mmm… Not so good. Well, I suppose that, by now, they'll have found out without a doubt. In any case, for a while I believed that the killers didn't know that they had killed Thérèse."

"And now?"

"Now I think that they knew who they were killing."

"But what…"

"Thérèse was involved with some people who wanted the secret of the text. She was supposed to get it for them from me but she didn't want to betray me. In the end, something went wrong and they killed her."

"Is this connected to the French investment firm that she worked for?"

"Bonsans? No. They wanted it too, but I don't think that they killed her."

"What?"

"There was someone else involved. Someone here in America. Someone here in this town."

"But who?"

"Can't tell you yet. I only suspect."

"What about Hakim Taflon?" Ben asked.

Marie seemed surprised. "How do you know his name?" she asked.

"He was checking out my boat and the police picked him up. They're still holding him."

Marie fell silent for a moment. "It will be bad for him," she said.

"What's his connection in this mess?"

"I'm not sure."

"Why was he in your apartment the night Thérèse was killed?"

"We talk enough," she said as she tried to curl up next to Ben.

"Not by half," said Ben as he stood up and went to the living room with his cognac. "And you owe me two hundred and fifty dollars," he said on his way to the couch.

"Two hundred forty," came the response. "And I'm sorry. I knew that it wouldn't be safe to use a credit or cash card after Maine so I needed some cash reserve."

"Cash reserve," mumbled Ben. "My cash, your reserve."

Ben sat on the couch in the half-light of the living room working on his cognac. It dawned on him that his initial impression of Marie at the faculty cocktail reception was absolutely correct. She was trouble. Even if he could get her to talk more now, she, very likely, would tell him only what she wanted him to tell the police. Of what she had told him already, how much was true? There was no way to tell. He poured himself another cognac from the bottle which he had left on the coffee table. He hated being taken advantage of. Damn her. And yet, he couldn't deny that he had felt a great relief when he saw her again and knew for sure that she wasn't dead. It was more than relief. He couldn't say that he loved her but he certainly wanted to help her, protect her, hold her. Shit.

After a few moments, Marie silently stepped over the arm of the couch and took a seat beside him. She moved like a cat. He first sensed her presence from the depression he felt in the cushion of the couch. Just like a cat. In the light drifting into the room from the street, he could make out that she was dressed in one of his shirts. Her hair was still damp from the shower.

"I know that I frustrate you, but I have to do this my way," she said in an attempt to apologize. "Hakim sometimes did jobs for Thérèse's company."

"What kind of jobs?"

"I don't know. Honestly, I don't know. Thérèse had him contact me to help him find someone here in America. He came up from Boston, slept over one night, and left. I never saw him again after he left that afternoon you and I met."

"Who was he looking for?"

"Rawlings."

"What, George Rawlings?"

"They, Bonsans and Thérèse, didn't know I was working for George. They were looking for Rawlings, I think, because he's an expert in the field. Thérèse recognized the name of the university and told Hakim to contact me."

She Blew into the Room

"But what good would contacting Rawlings do?"

"It would be useless, I know," said Marie, "and I told Hakim so. I already knew more about the text than George did."

"So what happened?"

"He said that if he didn't follow through with what he'd been asked to do, he would be in trouble. I helped him make an appointment to see Rawlings and he left when you and I arrived."

"And you don't think that he might have killed Thérèse?" asked Ben.

"No, not Hakim. At worst he was told to steal the text."

"Might he have been the one who searched my place?"

"Your place?"

"Yes, that night someone turned my house upside down looking for something."

"Well, it could have been Hakim. He had seen you and somehow could have found out where you lived. If he found nothing in my apartment he might have assumed that you had the text."

"Not a bad assumption under the circumstances. Can you tell me what happened that night?"

"That's about all I know. Early that next morning, Thérèse arrived from Boston. After a long talk, I left the apartment to do some errands. When I returned, I found Thérèse with a knife in her chest. I thought that she had been killed by mistake. The place was a mess so I was sure that they were looking for the text. I panicked. I fixed my hair to look more like Thérèse, knowing that everyone would assume that the dead person was me. I took her backpack and, with the key, found her rental car. I drove around for a while until I remembered that you said that you had a boat so I went down to the marina. I found your car and I waited. Soon you came out of *Emma* and left. I picked *Emma's* lock and hid inside."

Marie moved closer to Ben. She took his upper arm in both hands and lightly placed her head on his shoulder.

"That's all I know about what happened," she said. "Honest."

Ben felt his anger recede. He fought it, reminding himself of how she had used him. And was probably still using him. It was a losing battle.

"You said that you have to do this your way," said Ben. "What, exactly, are you doing?"

Marie was silent for a moment. "I can't just sit around and do nothing and trust that the police will figure everything out. I will learn who is behind this. And I will kill them. Like they killed Thérèse."

Her low measured voice was enough to convince Ben that she might be able to pull it off. "Can't you find out who killed her and tell the police?"

"And then maybe they don't make justice."

"Do you think Rawlings was involved?" he asked.

"I don't know. I have trouble believing that George would do something like this, but too many things lead back to the Rawlings house," she said.

"I know. And I feel the same way, George isn't a killer. It just doesn't make sense. Does your family back in France know what's going on?"

"Why do you ask?"

"Well if one of my daughters was killed and the other was in danger, I'd like to know."

"Yes, I've talked to Papá. I was afraid that it would kill him but he's stronger than I thought."

"Maybe you should keep yourself safe so that he doesn't lose another."

"Ben?" she said and paused.

She Blew into the Room

"What is it?"

Marie turned around on the couch so that she was facing Ben, her knees on the back of the couch, her arms around his neck, her head on his chest.

"I know that you're upset and I don't want you to be angry with me," she said. "I need you. You're the only friend I've got now." She began to cry in muffled tones.

Ben was ready to question her on her definition of friend, but decided against it. He instinctively put his arms around Marie to comfort her. She felt soft and fragile. He was toast.

"Ben, I need you. And I want you. I understand if you don't want—"

He stopped her with a kiss planted hard on her mouth. She responded and he dragged her across his lap and pressed her into the couch. Their legs were entangled in an awkward fashion but it didn't seem to matter. She unbuttoned his shirt and undid his pants while they were still locked in a kiss. She pushed him back up into a sitting position and slid off his lap onto the floor in front of him. She pulled down his pants and briefs and kissed his rising erection. Then she stood up, unbuttoned her shirt, and climbed onto his lap. He buried his head between her breasts as she slipped him inside of her. He grabbed her hips, pulled them down, and thrust upward hard. She gave a muffled cry. Ben realized that his anger and passion were making him lose control.

"Sorry," he whispered.

"Don't be sorry. And don't stop," she said.

He thrust again and again. At sometime in the future, he thought, we will have to make slow, gentle love. But sometime in the future. Not tonight.

Twenty minutes later they lay naked and spent on the couch, Ben on his back, Marie beside him with her head on his chest. He softly stroked the back of her head.

"Sorry about the rough love," he said.

"Don't be. I felt the same way. That's just where we are at the moment."

"I realize that we hardly know each other, but when I thought that you were dead, I had such a terrible lost feeling. I can't explain it."

"Don't try to explain. I think we are good together. I especially enjoyed sailing with you. You learn many things about people when sailing."

"Yes, our little trip down east was trying and confusing, but you're great to sail with, in whatever reincarnation you take."

"When this is over, I would like to take a real sailing trip with you on your little *Emma*."

"Can't think of anything I'd like more. Maybe the Caribbean."

"Tell me," she said. "When we were sailing, you really thought that I was Thérèse, correct?"

"Well, yes, it was only after you jumped ship that I started having doubts."

"Jumped ship? You mean abandoning you?"

"Yes, old English term."

"Okay but you were starting to be attracted to this Thérèse on your boat. I could tell. And with me only recently dead."

"I don't know how to explain it. Somehow you were a complete replacement for yourself. I couldn't look at you without thinking that Marie was still alive."

They were quiet for a while.

"Marie, I wish I could convince you not to avenge your sister's murder by yourself. These people are killers. They know who you are. Even if you're successful, you might end up in jail."

"Please, let's not talk about this. I know what I'm doing."

"But will you let me help you?"

"No. If I'm successful, then the police will probably find out that you were involved. I'm willing to take the risk for me but not for you. It's better this way."

"I don't want to lose you again."

"Not to worry. You won't." She raised herself up on her elbow and gave him a kiss. "By the way, do you know that you have a spirit in your bedroom?"

"Yes, his name is Ezekiel. Lost at sea about two hundred years ago."

"Ezekiel, what a great New England name. Do you talk to him?"

"No, we're just two bachelors going about our business without bothering each other."

"That's nice," she said as she gave him another kiss.

The morning light brought Ben into the waking world. He found himself in bed. He rolled over and could smell Marie's scent on the pillow next to him. As he was getting his eyes open, he reached out to put his arm around her but it fell on an empty bed. Marie was gone. He listened for a moment to see if she might be in the kitchen or the bathroom, but the house was quiet. He put on a robe and stumbled to the kitchen. There, next to the coffee maker was a note.

Ben,
Sorry but I have to do it my way.
And sorry for the money.
Just add it to my tab.
      Love, M.

Her tab? Ben returned to the living room and found his wallet next to a pile of clothes on the coffee table. Empty except for ten dollars. He remembered the four hundred dollars he had just taken out of the ATM and mentally tried to add $240 to $390. He struggled a bit and gave up. Mathematicians have trouble with arithmetic. In any case she owed him a lot of money. She had done it again. His immediate reaction was anger but it quickly ebbed as the clothes strewn about the living room reminded him of the night before. A smile tried to cross his face. At least she isn't just after my body, he thought; she's after my money too. Then, his mood quickly changed again to one of concern. Marie was out there alone, trying catch up with some dangerous people. People who would probably kill her if they had the chance.

A knock at the front door broke into his thoughts. He opened the door to a smiling Detective Townsend.

"Mind if I come in?"

"I was just about to make some coffee. Would you like some?"

Townsend nodded and they made their way through the living room to the kitchen. Ben braced himself for some sarcastic comment on the clothes lying about in the living room but none came. Townsend just quietly sighed.

They were silent while Ben started the coffee maker. He wondered about the purpose of Townsend's visit. He thought of Marie and wondered if he should tell Townsend of her visit. He couldn't decide whether it would help her or not. In any case, they lived in a small town and there was a high probability that Townsend would find out anyway. Finally Ben broke the silence.

"I had a visitor last night. The sister of the girl that was killed."

"Yes, I know. Marie?" Townsend responded with a statement in the form of a question.

"How did you know?"

Townsend smiled, "One of our patrolmen checking on your house saw a woman with a backpack leave your house about four in the morning. I assumed that it was her."

"Marie and not Thérèse?"

"Yes, we've positively identified the victim as Thérèse LaFontaine. We have limited resources in our quaint small town but we do know how to do police work."

"Never doubted it for a minute," said Ben.

"In any case, I'm glad that you volunteered the information. The state of your living room leaves little doubt as to who our patrolman saw."

Ben flushed, "I tried to get her to come into your custody, but she's on a mission and feels that she has to act on her own."

"She's likely to get herself killed too."

"I'm afraid that you're right," said Ben as he handed Townsend his coffee.

Ben offered cream and sugar but the detective refused as if the idea of adulterating black coffee was a sin.

"Is Taflon still in custody?"

"Indeed he is. The Boston PD has officially asked us to hold him on drug trafficking charges. They'll pick him up whenever we're done with him."

"That's good of them, but what do you expect—"

"I know he's involved some way in the murder. I don't know how yet, but I feel that if we can sweat him a little more we can get what we need."

"Rubber hoses in the back room?"

Townsend laughed. "No, unfortunately, those days went out long ago. Now it's mind games. Constant pressure. Making him think we know things that we only suspect. Playing on his fear of being framed for something he didn't do."

"You don't think he killed Thérèse?"

"No, but I think he knows who did. Or, at least, what was going on that night and who the players were."

"I wish I could be of help."

"Well, you are, of sorts. I don't mean to use you as bait, but I think that, sooner or later, the responsible parties will come back to you."

"Back to me?"

"Yes, I see it this way. It's appearing more and more likely that they were after the text and probably still are. In any case they can't know who has it and you're one of the likely candidates. We have Hakim Taflon locked up and if they can't find Marie, you will be the only lead they have."

"Interesting."

"I wouldn't blame you if you wanted to disappear for awhile, but if you're willing to stay, we'll keep close tabs on you. No guarantees, of course. However, I think that we can protect you. Besides, aren't you one of Ma's martial arts guys?" Townsend said with a smile.

"I am. Just a little old and slow. Don't worry. I'll stay. The best way to protect Marie is to get to the bottom of this mess."

"Good man. I thought you'd see it that way."

Townsend finished his coffee and rose to leave.

"Put my cell number in your phone so you can reach me quickly if you suspect any visitors."

"It's already there," said Ben.

"Go back to parking in your driveway so that your car can be seen from the street. That way we'll know where you are and so will they. Right in front of the garage would be good. Call me if you sense anything out of the ordinary. And good luck."

Detective Townsend left Ben to ponder his situation. Even if Marie were safe, he would still be willing to serve as bait. The image of Thérèse's brutal murder had never left him. And probably never would. He had never thought of himself as brave, but he was involved and he was angry. His own safety would be secondary until the killers were brought to justice.

Ben spent the next couple of days at his office in the university, tidying up some of the yearend loose ends that he had left when he took *Emma* to Maine. On Thursday he noticed a penciled-in star on his calendar. An attempt to remind himself of the Third Thursday Group. The Group, as they called themselves, were musicians who met every third Thursday of the month at Peckham's Pub. The pub had a small raised stage on which were hosted open-mike activities and even paid bands from time to time. But the stage was reserved, on the third Thursday of every month for The Group. How it all evolved, Ben couldn't remember exactly, but, if pressed, he would probably mention the night two years before when he stopped by the pub after a guitar lesson. He had had no intention of performing but a singer and a pianist encouraged him and, with Bill Peckham's approval, they took the stage. It was a fun night. Afterward Peckham asked Ben if he would like to make it a monthly event. Perhaps it was late in the evening after too many drinks but Ben agreed and the Third Thursday Group became a scheduled happening. Many types of music were tried but currently The Group featured mostly Latin music, classical or traditional, sometimes jazz and even pop. Ben was a regular, along with Pete, a lanky stand-up bass player, and Phil, a percussionist from the conservatory. Other members of The Group floated in and out but there were usually five or six in the ensemble every third Thursday. One of the best things about a small university town is that amazing talent can just float in.

With everything that had happened in the past few days Ben had considered skipping this meeting but he didn't want to disappoint his fellow group mates and the mood at the pub was usually mellow and might calm him down. He arrived with his guitar at eight o'clock. Phil arrived at the same time with his cart of percussion instruments. Since they were never sure how the music would unfold during the course of the evening, Phil wanted to be ready for anything. Ben and Phil ordered drinks and joined the others on stage. Pete introduced them to two new members—Raul, a Brazilian acoustic guitarist, and Karina, a strikingly beautiful Venezuelan singer. Ben smiled as he wondered why Venezuelan women always seemed to be good looking. Perhaps they drown the ugly ones at birth.

Karina had brought some sheet music, mostly old standards by Jobim, Bonfá, and Baden Powell, which she and Ben used. Phil, Raul and Pete didn't seem to need written music. The impromptu ensemble blended well from the start. Since some of the music was new to Ben, he concentrated on cording as accompaniment while Raul did most of the embellishment. Karina's voice was clear with wonderful overtones and a touch of melancholy. An appreciative crowd, mostly third Thursday regulars, filled the pub.

During their break the pub's owner, Bill, sent over a round of drinks. Karina seemed surprised. "Why this?" she asked.

"This is our pay," said Ben as he toasted the group.

"So now we're professional musicians?" Karina laughed.

"If you're not already, you could be," said Ben. "Are you from the conservatory?"

"No, I'm in medical school. Soon to be a doctor."

Ben laughed and shook his head. Some people have everything, he thought.

"What about you, Raul?"

"Medical school, too, although I'm pleased to be able to call myself a professional musician now. And the rest of you?"

"Well, Phil, there, is a professor in the conservatory and the timpanist in the New England Philharmonic. I'm a professor in the math department. And Pete is our local pharmacist."

"This has been great fun. Could we join you again sometime?" asked Karina.

"You two are always welcome," said Pete.

"Karina, do you usually sing Brazilian music?" asked Phil.

"Yes, it just suits me better."

"How about Villa-Lobos?" asked Ben.

"Yes, I love his music. My favorite of his for voice is the aria from the Bachianas Brasileires No. 5 but I think that it might be too far out for a pub crowd. And besides I didn't bring the music."

"You might be wrong about this crowd and I don't need the music. This is one piece I know."

The rest of the group took a rest while Ben and Karina performed the aria, a haunting, flowing melody with intricate guitar accompaniment. The audience was silent. Imagine a crowded pub where nobody is talking. Karina's voice was perfect for the aria. When she finished, the crowd burst into applause and most of them rose to their feet. Karina was beaming. She leaned over Ben, who was still seated, to give him a kiss on the top of his head. Ben was happy that he had decided to join the group that night; for a few minutes he had actually forgotten about the murder and the mess he was in.

The next day Ben took his place at the oral exam of his graduate assistant, Sid, with Professors Irslinger and Crowley. As predicted, Irslinger tried to put the fear of God into the young doctoral candidate but Sid's calm and considered responses carried the day.

When Irslinger brought up Cantor's paradox, Sid dove in and lead the discussion back to the Burali-Forti paradox before Irslinger could get there. Irslinger was visibly frustrated. At the end of the two-hour session, Sid was asked to leave the room while the committee deliberated as was the tradition. More fear of God. However, the outcome was obvious, even to Irslinger and, two minutes later, Sid was called back into the room and congratulated. Sid was elated and patted Ben on the back as he shook his hand. Ben stopped by George Rawlings' office but was informed that George had not been there since the murder. Probably still in shock, thought Ben. Or still in Martiniville.

Ben went to Professor Hameister's office as requested. Friedrich Hameister, an ancient German once famous for his contributions to number theory, was the head of the Math Department and had expressed dismay over the furor caused by Ben's multiple choice final exam. The undergraduates called him Herr Professor Hamster. Not to his face, of course. There were solid rumors on campus that Hameister had been a fighter pilot in World War II, on the German side. Some pictures in his office, especially one of a young blond man standing proudly by a Messerschmitt ME-109, seemed to corroborate the story. Ben tried to do the math. If Hameister were 17 in 1945, he would have to be close to eighty now. He could be. Hard to tell and no one on the staff was about to ask him. Fascinating story if true. What was the probability of a German fighter pilot surviving the war? Near zero, one would think. Ben liked Hameister despite his gruff manner. However, every time Ben saw Hameister he couldn't get the image of hamsters wearing flight helmets out of his mind.

Professor Hameister wanted to know more about the exam but had not seen it so Ben ran back to his office and returned with a copy. One page, twenty questions. The professor adjusted his reading glasses and started reading the exam. His normally serious demeanor softened. As he read on, a smile started to form. He stopped for a moment and looked at Ben as if seeing him for the first time. Hameister said nothing, however, and returned to the exam. Finally, nearing the end of the exam, he broke out in laughter and dropped the exam onto his desk.

"No wonder they claimed that you tricked them. This exam is a mine field. And beautifully done."

"The best students did well," Ben said in his defense, "but most of the others charged ahead with a false sense of security. Hopefully, they've learned to be more careful."

"Yes, and not to be so readily tricked."

The interview was over. Hameister laughed as he took Ben to the door and ushered him out, closing the door behind him. As he went down the hall, Ben could still hear the old man laughing through the closed door.

Kung Fu

Ben just had time to pick up his gear and head to the Kung Fu Center for Martial Arts. His weekly pole training sessions with Master Ma were usually private, but tonight Ma introduced two young men in their early twenties. They were new brown belts in the open hand forms and were just beginning their weapons training. The four of them spent an hour on one-person *katas*, Ma focusing on Ben while the two young men shadowed the moves in the background. Then, another half hour on two-person *katas*. First a slow motion demonstration by Ma and Ben. Then Ben worked with one of the young men while Ma worked with the other. The session ended with a short mock combat between Ma and Ben. "Just to keep you sharp," as Ma said.

Ben stopped at the ATM, then bought some groceries and drove home. He parked by the side of the house in front of the detached garage. Entering through the kitchen door, he put the bags on the counter and flipped on the lights. No lights. Still adjusting to the darkness from the head lights of his car, he moved to the living room and reached for the light switch on the wall just outside the kitchen. Before his hand touched the switch, he received a kick to the ribs under his outstretched arm. Holy shit, he thought, they're here. And that was a side kick, more associated with Tae Kwan Do than with Kung Fu. The powerful kick knocked him backward in the direction of the sofa. There, he felt the presence of a second assailant and, as he turned, he received a blow to the head just above the eye. Probably a back fist. Another kick from the first guy, this one landing on his shoulder and knocking him onto the sofa. How many are they? Ben bounced off the sofa in the direction of the closet by the front door. His eyes were becoming accustomed to the darkness. He pulled open the closet door in time to block another punch. Not planned, but very effective. Fist on wood. Ben could hear a sharp intake of breath from his assailant followed by "*Merde.*" That must have smarted.

Ben reached inside the closet and found a pole he kept there for defense purposes although he never really thought that it would be needed in their small New England town. Ben made a strong horizontal sweep with the pole in order to clear some space to move. The end of the pole connected to something solid, probably a head. The only light in the room was filtering in from the street through the front windows that were at Ben's back. Not a good place to be. Ben made some vertical strokes to clear a path and bolted to the opposite side of the room. Now he could see his assailants dimly silhouetted. Advantage, Slade. He could hear Ma's voice in his head, "More than one opponent? Dispatch, dispatch. You don't have time to come back a second time." Okay, I will dispatch with vigor. Don't have to kill them, just make sure that they don't get up again very soon. "Clear the mind, relax, and focus. Let your reactions control the flow." Okay, got that part. The endless repetition of *katas* made the movements second nature. "Never underestimate your opponent." Okay, I won't. These guys are pretty good. Now let's see what they've got. Ben relaxed and waited.

Another side kick, launched at Ben's head, was easily blocked with the pole. Perhaps blocked is not the right description since Ben met the kick on the ankle with such force that he was pretty sure that something broke. And it wasn't his pole. Before the leg came down Ben made a sweep with the other end of the pole to the exposed groin. Never thought that those high side kicks were good for much. Almost as one motion, Ben reversed the sweep of the pole and caught the second man on the side of the head as he advanced to take his fallen comrade's place. The second man fell like a rag doll on top of the first. Suddenly, there was no movement except for some labored breathing.

Ben paused motionless for a full minute and convinced himself that there were only two. Then he went to the kitchen pantry to turn the lights back on at the breaker panel. The lights revealed two men in a heap on the living room floor. One was out cold but the other was still moving. Ben poked him in the temple with the end of the pole and put him out as well. No use to take any chances. He found his cell phone and a beer, sat on the sofa with his pole while he called Detective Townsend.

"Detective Townsend, here."

"This is Ben Slade. The bait worked, they're here."

"Are you okay?"

"Fine."

"What do you mean they're here? Where are they?"

"There are two thugs here bleeding on my living room rug. You're welcome to come collect them."

"Be right there. Don't take any chances. They are dangerous people."

"Well, they don't look too dangerous at the moment."

"We'll be right there."

Good to his word, within five minutes Detective Townsend came through the back door as three uniformed cops entered through the front. Ben remained seated on the sofa, still drinking his beer. Ben thought that it was remarkable that he felt so calm given the life and death contest that had just transpired. At some level he had trained for that moment for many years. Townsend took in the situation in an instant.

"They were waiting for you when you came home?" he asked Ben.

"Yes, in the dark. They have some kind of karate training. High kicks and all that."

"But you had a stick," said Townsend looking at the six-foot pole across Ben's lap.

"That's right. I hit them with a stick."

"Looks like you hit them pretty hard. We'll have to hospitalize one of them at least. Did you break his ankle?"

"Appears so."

"Did they say anything?"

"Ouch, I think."

"Very funny. Did they ask you anything?"

"No, they just started beating on me."

The uniformed policemen cuffed the two men and emptied their pockets. No weapons, just cash and French passports.

"Damn," said Townsend checking the two men's clothes labels.

"What's wrong?" asked Ben.

"Frenchies most likely but their passports are probably fake. Now the FBI will have to be involved for sure."

Ben was puzzled, "Isn't that a good thing?"

"Sort of like inviting the Romans in to make peace. They don't go home again. I don't want to spend the rest of this investigation taking orders from some snot-nosed kid from the Boston bureau."

Ben chuckled as he shook his head.

"And the other problem," Townsend added in a lighter tone, "is that we're running out of cells at the local jail. We'll have to find another place for the town drunk to sleep it off. Better get that eye looked at. Looks like you zigged when you should have zagged."

"They hit me in the dark. I never saw—" responded Ben before he realized that Townsend was pulling his leg.

"Don't worry, Professor, you were terrific," said Townsend. "Wish I could've been there to watch."

"Just to watch?"

"Doesn't look like you needed any help."

The police force departed with their two prisoners who were just starting to come around. The uniformed cops were none too gentle and Ben felt a little sorry for the man with the broken ankle. Not too sorry, just a little.

Ben put some hydrogen peroxide and a butterfly on the cut above his left eye. Not bad enough for stitches but it was going to generate a magnificent shiner. Next he tried to clean up the blood on the carpet. He put away his groceries, cooked some pasta with meat sauce, and opened a bottle of San Giovese to make dinner more interesting.

Ben tried to watch TV but soon realized that he couldn't stop his mind from wandering. At the first commercial, when he asked himself what he was watching and found he couldn't answer, he turned off the TV. He got out his guitar and started to practice but he couldn't concentrate. Too much going on.

First, there was the excitement of the attack. He had studied martial arts since he was a teenager and had been through many contests and tournaments, but he had never used his skill in anger, as they say. Well, not appropriate for martial arts since anger is supposed to be removed from the equation. But in his whole life, he had never used his skill to defend himself knowing that he was in danger, perhaps mortal danger. There had been confrontations in bars and on the streets where his confidence and calm had probably averted physical violence. It was true that he had never really felt endangered in such situations. Somehow his training would carry him through. And the training had carried him through. He smiled as he remembered Ma's voice, "dispatch, dispatch" during the short battle. Yes, the training had worked.

He had been tested and had been victorious. With only a cut and a few bruises to show for it.

Second, in the morass of possible scenarios that might have led to Thérèse's death, the French connection was becoming clear. The appearance of the French thugs almost proved the proposition that Thérèse was killed for the text. Too much coincidence to believe otherwise. Marie probably knows who was involved and what happened, but, clearly, she's not talking. She only drops in to sleep with me and empty my wallet. Then there's George. George probably knows more that he has let on. Ben picked up the phone.

"Hello, George, this is Ben."

"Ben.....Ben, how are you?" George sounded disoriented.

"Did I wake you up?"

"No...no, not really. Just sitting here thinking...and drinking."

"Mind if I come over and have a drink with you?"

"Good idea. I've been rattling around in this mausoleum all by myself."

"Be right there."

Ben backed out of his driveway and covered the distance to the Rawlings house in five minutes. George met him at the door. He looked terrible. He reminded Ben of one of the bums in a local production of *Waiting for Godot*.

"What happened to you?" asked George.

"Walked into two thugs from France."

George ushered him into the study with no reaction to Ben's comment.

"Martinis, okay?" asked George. "I'm on a roll."

"Sure, one of your martinis is just what I need. I take it that Frieda is still in Europe."

"Yup. She called early this morning...from Zurich, I think. Well, somewhere in Switzerland. Be back soon, she said. Better get this place cleaned up," he said looking around to assess the mess.

"Two thugs, you said. What did they want?"

"Don't know," said Ben. "We didn't get that far."

"Where are they now?"

"In the custody of the local police. One in the hospital, the other in jail, I believe."

"You did them in?"

"That I did."

"Kung Fu and all that?"

"Right, maybe I got lucky."

"All those years of practice should amount to something," said George. "From France you said?"

"French passports. French clothes labels."

"Mmm...Too many French actors in this drama."

"I couldn't agree more...George, I've got a question for you that you may not like."

George sat down behind his desk, his habitual spot, and motioned Ben to a chair. "Shoot," he said.

"When I asked you a few days ago about Hakim Taflon coming to your house, I got the feeling that you were holding something back. Can you tell me what was going on?"

George sat motionless for a moment before pivoting his chair to face Ben.

"I said that Taflon asked if I knew where Thérèse was, I believe."

"That's right, you did."

"What I didn't tell you, or the police, was that he also asked for Frieda."

"What?...Why the—"

"I have no idea. Honestly, I have no idea."

"Marie told me that Taflon did odd jobs for Thérèse's company, that Bonsans group. Does Frieda have connections with them?"

"Not that I know of. You said that Marie told you. When was that? When did you see her last?"

Ben paused. He was starting to wonder just how much information he should be giving George.

"I don't really remember when," said Ben, "perhaps it was when she was on the boat."

"Then you're sure that it was Marie and not Thérèse?"

"Yes, Marie is still alive. Thérèse was killed."

"And the police know?"

"Yes, of course."

"Where is Marie now?"

Ben decided not to let George know that she was probably still in town or when he had seen her last. He felt guilty about deceiving his long-time friend, but he wasn't sure that he could trust him completely.

"I don't know," said Ben.

They sat with their thoughts for several minutes. George absent mindedly rotated his desk chair back and forth while staring out the window. Ben watched him wondering if his old friend could be a villain. Of course, he wasn't a murderer, but Ben reasoned that Marie would be safer if no one knew where she was.

As Ben's thoughts turned to Marie, he felt the need to return home. Perhaps she would come back. Perhaps she would leave a message. In any case he wasn't getting much information from George.

Ben rose and said, "Thanks for the drink, George. I've got to do a pole demonstration at the martial arts tournament tomorrow night so I'd better get some sleep."

He drove home to an empty house and crawled into an empty bed.

Surveillance

The next morning Ben downed some coffee and drove to the police station. In the window of the bakery next to the police station he happened to see a poster announcing the karate tournament. He winced as he noticed a note near the bottom of poster:

"Kung Fu Pole Demonstration by Ben Slade." Should have told Master Ma that my name in lights wasn't necessary, he thought.

Detective Townsend was in his office and he seemed pleased to see Ben.

"Ah, Professor, to what do we owe the pleasure of your visit? Here, take a seat. Ed, bring the professor some coffee. Black, one sugar."

Ben was surprised that Townsend knew how he took his coffee, then he realized that the detective, by habit, observed all details and forgot nothing.

"Thanks, I wanted to learn what you've found out about my night visitors. And I have a bit of new information for you."

"Great," said Townsend, "I'll start. We found their rental car in the neighborhood. The driver's license for the rental yielded more information than their passports, which honestly, aren't even very good fakes. I was up early this morning to deal with the French during their office hours. These two birds are both from Marseille and have records at Interpol."

"Are they wanted by the French?"

"At the moment, only for the possession of fake French passports. In any case, one is in isolation at the hospital. The doctor said you really did a job on his ankle. We put the other one in an adjoining cell, we have only two, next to Taflon under surveillance. Secret surveillance."

"And what did they talk about?"

"Nothing. *Rien*."

"Then, what—"

Townsend was obviously enjoying his game. "They completely avoided each other. Not a word all night. Imagine two thugs from Marseille and they ignore each other all night. They *have* to know one another."

"I see what you mean."

"They probably work for the same person or organization. And Taflon has become despondent. Hardly eats, although I must admit we don't exactly serve French cuisine here."

"He's afraid of having the murder pinned on him?" asked Ben.

"Exactly. Nobody has made a move to get him released or to represent him. I think that he's been cut adrift and he knows it. Now, what do you have for me?"

"You mentioned that, when you questioned George Rawlings about Taflon, you felt that he was lying."

"Did and do," said the detective.

"Taflon asked him about Thérèse—"

"So he said."

"And then he asked for George's wife, Frieda. George didn't want to tell you until he understood why."

Townsend held up his hand to pause the conversation. He rocked back in his chair and stared at the ceiling. Ben realized that the detective must have at least half a dozen possible scenarios racing through his mind. The small office was silent for several minutes except for the usual bustle of activity in the police station at large. Finally Townsend rocked forward and fixed his gaze on Ben.

"I know that you're an old friend of George Rawlings. I appreciate your telling me what you've learned. It may be important, but I must admit, none of the pieces fit together at the moment. The text as motive, but the wrong girl murdered. The Rawlings' involvement, now both of them. The French mafia connection, which I'm afraid, we've not seen the last of. And the part that bothers me most—"

"What's that?"

"According to your statement, Marie called someone to tell them excitedly in French that the mystery had been solved…Who the hell was it?"

"I thought that you checked the phone records."

Townsend laughed. "Of course we did. She called a new cell phone belonging to a bogus person living at a bogus address. But, you said she knew the number from memory."

"She did, but why is the phone call so important?" asked Ben.

"That phone call probably started the chain of events that led to her sister's death. Not Marie's fault necessarily, but she almost certainly knows, at this point, who was responsible. And is out to get them on her own. Meanwhile, we're still in the dark, testing suppositions. I've now got at least four different scenarios, each equally probable given the facts that we know for sure. It's a real mess of a case."

"Has the FBI been notified?"

"The *suits* are in evidence."

Detective Townsend nodded through the interior windows of his office to a desk in a corner of the main lobby occupied by a young man and a young lady, both in dark suits. A uniformed policeman was in attendance shaking his head in agreement with whatever one of the *suits* was saying.

"They shouldn't get in the way too much," said Townsend. "So far, they haven't accepted the 'text-as-motive' hypothesis so they're off on another track. Maybe French baroque poetry doesn't play to their strengths."

"The Marseille mafia connection must have caught their interest."

"Indeed, but Taflon's suspected drug dealings in Boston have them salivating for an international drug bust. The kind of thing that makes a career for a young agent."

"Can't you get them on the right track?" asked Ben.

Townsend raised his hands in mock frustration. "God knows, I tried, but I'm just a small town detective who's obviously out of his depth."

Ben smiled. "Well, for all we know, they might be right too."

"Oh, they probably *are* right, but drug trafficking has nothing to do with the murder. The murder happened on *my* watch, in *my* town and *I'm* going to make sure that those responsible pay for it."

Ben realized that he had an appointment at the university conservatory. He drove home to pick up his guitar and headed to the office of Celso Machado, a Brazilian guitarist of some renown, who was on staff as a professor of classical guitar but also taught private lessons to a select few. Ben felt fortunate to have arranged a monthly slot with Machado to improve his technique and to gain access to music of composers he wouldn't have otherwise discovered. The Argentinian Cardoso and the Venezuelan Borges were two such finds.

Ben arrived early and took a seat in the small waiting room outside Machado's office. He could hear the perfectly even repeated notes of the *Recuerdos de la Alhambra*. He must be practicing, thought Ben. Then he heard, "No, more like this." And the same passage was repeated in perfectly even fashion. At least Ben couldn't tell the difference. The lesson continued with Ben's building respect for the student's ability. Finally, the lesson ended and the office door opened. Out came a twelve-year-old kid who was thanking the professor profusely for his time. Given that a child's hands are usually not big enough to handle most of classical guitar techniques until they are eleven or twelve, this kid had mastered a lot in a very short period of time.

Celso smiled at Ben as if reading his mind. "Come in Ben." And once inside the office he said, "He's good isn't he?"

"Fantastic," said Ben with a creeping feeling of inadequacy.

"Both his parents are in the conservatory. String players. But the boy wants to learn the guitar so I'm filling in."

"Talent must be in his genes," said Ben.

"Mmm...Hard to make the nature vs. nurture argument since he has both."

"Yes, and so did Mozart and Beethoven. Oh well, I guess that the rest of us just have to struggle."

Celso laughed. "You struggle well enough. By the way, that was a great performance of the Villa-Lobos aria last Thursday night."

"You were there? I didn't see you."

"The place was packed. I wasn't there long but I did catch you and that beautiful singer. Remarkable voice. She didn't exactly sound Brazilian. Do you know where she's from?"

"She's a Venezuelan medical student."

"Well, she had the audience in the palm of her hand. You could hear a pin drop."

"Yes, it was a great crowd. You should join us sometime, third Thursday of every month. We get free drinks."

"Just might do that," Celso said with a smile. "Now let's see what you've done to Torroba's Sonatina."

After his lesson Ben went back to his office to finish some end of semester details. It was such a lovely warm day for a change that he decided to leave his car where it was and walk down to the marina to check on *Emma*. The events that had taken place after his arrival from Maine hadn't allowed him the time to put things back in order.

The town's founding fathers had allocated a prime spot for the university, situating it on a hill overlooking the harbor and adjoining town. Over the years the university had grown down the hill toward the harbor leaving only a small park as a buffer. Now that spring was in evidence the park was alive with students, some actually studying for that last exam but most playing ultimate Frisbee or just lying in the grass. Music was provided by a couple playing a recorder and guitar. Ah, spring. As Ben crossed the park, a Frisbee zinged past his head.

"Hello, Professor Slade," a cheerful voice rang out.

Ben turned to respond, "Hello, Alyssa, all finished?"

She ran over and picked up the Frisbee, "Yup, it's Miller time."

Alyssa was dressed in cutoff jeans short shorts and tank top, as were most of the young ladies in the park. During the long winter, dress was generally mukluks and long quilted down coats reminiscent of the Russian great coats that Peter the Great tried to suppress. The transformation to summer attire was striking. While the men sported a motley collection of baggy shorts, flip-flops and t-shirts, the women seemingly dressed to the same code and to great effect. Ben mused that the students seemed to be getting younger every year.

"Do you know that it's springtime, Professor?" she said with a laugh. The group of girls waiting for the Frisbee gave a muffled chuckle.

Ben realized that he was still wearing what he had worn more or less all winter: Sagging tweed jacket, kakis, and light hiking boots. In defense he pulled the lapel of his jacket and said, "Yes, this is about to come off."

"And some shorts?"

"Yes, shorts and sandals."

Play resumed and Ben crossed the rest of the park to the marina. He was more or less accustomed to being the subject of flirtatious advances from the coeds. Generally the flirtations were playful and harmless, spawned by curiosity about the effectiveness of one's charm on an attractive mid-forties professor. However, last fall shortly after Christine had left, a young math major, Sri, made serious advances. Sri was, at least partially, of Indian descent with long black hair, dark skin, and a dynamite body. She somehow knew that his wife had left him and was doing everything she could to fill the void. Not recognizing how serious she was, Ben made the mistake of not putting a stop to her attentions until he returned home one evening and found her in his house waiting for him with cocktails, wearing nothing but his bathrobe. It almost worked. Somehow he resisted and managed to get the brokenhearted girl back into her clothes and out the door. He had felt righteous and honorable at the time although he still had the occasional dream about Sri of a definitely unrighteous nature.

Once again, he found *Emma* unlocked yet undisturbed. If Marie is making *Emma* one of her nesting places, that's fine with me, he thought. She must have others among her friends in the graduate student community. He spent the rest of the morning cleaning up and fixing minor problems. At lunch time he walked across the parking lot to the diner. Evie made an embarrassing show of sympathy, to the point of ignoring other customers. At first Ben thought that the sympathy was for his black eye, but it turned out that the current rumor around town was that Ben's girlfriend had been murdered. When Ben established that the murder victim was the sister of a young lady whom he had only recently met, Evie seemed quite relieved. Small towns, he thought.

Tournament

Ben fiddled around on the boat for a few more hours before returning home for a nap and an early light dinner. He collected his martial arts gear and headed for the university gym. The tournament was well underway. Ma's reputation drew contestants from around the state and beyond, some from well-known *dojos* in Boston. Ma was something of a maverick. The Chinese are usually reluctant to teach Kung Fu to non-Chinese. Ma not only taught Kung Fu to all creeds and colors, he encouraged competitions between his students and those of other martial arts schools. Instead of criticizing the Tae Kwan Do schools for converting a martial art into a sport, Ma engaged them and their students to 'increase learning' as he said. His annual tournament had grown in popularity and size over several years, becoming a major event on the Chamber of Commerce's calendar. The university had been convinced to provide the facilities. And Ma's management of the event and choice of judges promoted an atmosphere of fair play. May the best contestants win. And they usually did.

Ben put on his *gi* in the locker room and entered the gym where the main competition was still in progress. Ma nodded to him as he found his seat. The competitors seemed younger than ever. But, at the same time, they seemed more flexible, more agile, and faster. Flaws and omissions in training were obvious, but the skill level had definitely moved up a notch since Ben had been in these competitions. My god, he thought, these kids are bigger and better than when I was doing this stuff. And I'm sure that I remember myself as better than I really was.

Ben scanned the crowd. Probably six hundred spectators, not bad for a local event. Ma must be pleased. He noticed Detective

Townsend who was also watching the crowd instead of the competition. Another figure caught Ben's eye, a young lady in a hooded sweatshirt. Blond hair streamed out from under the hood and her face was partially hidden, so he couldn't tell for sure, but he thought that she might be Marie. "My god," he thought, "why would she take the chance of showing up here?"

He tried not to stare, but it was hard not to keep his eyes fixed on her. When he managed to look over the rest of the crowd, several rows behind the hooded figure, he found three men in dark clothes, close replicas of the two French thugs that had attacked him. They stood out in the crowd, seemingly disinterested in the event. They were not here to watch their nephew win the title.

Just as Ben was trying to decide what to do about Marie and the three men, the first half of the competition concluded and Master Ma signaled Ben to come forward. Ma made a short announcement about Ben's level of achievement and turned the floor over to him. Some of the spectators had already made for the restrooms, but as Ben started the long *kata*, many returned to watch. The speed of the six-foot pole swirling around his body made it difficult to picture how any attacker could be successful in penetrating the sphere created by its motion. And old Ben still showed fluidity and grace, making the *kata* a pleasure to watch. Ma stood by proudly. Ben was in the zone, he was alone in the *kata*.

When Ben finished, there was a reasonable applause. Evidently enough of the spectators appreciated what they had seen. Ben bowed and was joined by Ma with his pole. Ma's simple announcement, "Mock combat," started the next entertainment. Well, entertainment for some, a real contest for Ben. Ben had decided not to let this demonstration degenerate into a lesson in front of hundreds of people. He went at Ma with measured aggressiveness.

Too much aggression would certainly be his downfall, but he attacked with more force and ingenuity than was his custom. Ma immediately adjusted, retreating, moving side to side like a gazelle. The crowd was silenced in awe. Few had ever seen a demonstration with such speed and power. To most it appeared that the two participants were out to win, holding nothing back. The instant that Ben's attack paused, Ma took the initiative and Ben was forced into the role of backpedaling defender. Ma, who was surprised and pleased at Ben's approach, matched Ben's vigor exactly. The teacher, of course, could defeat the student almost at will and Ben was certainly conscious of the fact. Both combatants were skillful enough not to hurt each other.

At one point Ben became distracted for an instant by the hooded figure in the stands. That's all it took for Ma to dislodge Ben's pole which sailed up through the air and landed unceremoniously at the teacher's feet. The crowd took a breath as one. Without changing his stance or his grip on his pole, Ma placed his foot on Ben's pole, rolled it back like a soccer ball to the top of his foot, flipped it to Ben, and renewed his attack. The crowd cheered. The contest continued for several more minutes until Ma stepped back and held up his hand. It had been a strenuous demonstration and both men were trying to hide the fact that they were out of breath. They bowed to each other and then turned to the crowd and bowed. The crowd applauded and cheered. Most realized that they had been privileged to see something that they hadn't known existed. Ma put his arm around Ben and thanked him.

Ma looked at Ben's eye and asked, "You have trouble?"

"Yes, two thugs from France, but they're in jail now."

"Three more in audience."

"I saw them, but maybe they're not after me."

"Maybe. Take care."

Ma bowed again and returned to the microphone to start the second half of the tournament. Ben sat with Ma's students and watched the rest of the competition. Checking the stands, he noticed that the three men were still there, but the girl in the hooded sweatshirt was gone.

An hour later, the competition was over. A young Korean from a Boston *dojo* won first place but two of Ma's more advanced students placed second and fourth, so there was a general sense of celebration among the group. Ben accompanied them back to the locker room to change to his street clothes. Congratulating the contestants and receiving some congratulations himself, he went to his car in the parking lot. Most of spectators had left by this time so the parking lot was fairly empty. As Ben unlocked his car door, a black sedan pulled up alongside and the three unsavory-looking men from the tournament crowd jumped out. One of them had a gun in his hand.

"Get into the car," he said making sure that Ben saw the gun.

Ben was pretty sure that his pole would not carry the day against three men with at least one gun. *Thought that these things only happened in the movies.* Ben was still trying to decide what to do when the door to the gym burst open and a noisy crowd of tournament participants headed towards Ben and the thugs. They were Ma's students accompanied by Ma himself. They were laughing and talking, seemingly oblivious to what was going on in the parking lot. One of the thugs waved them off but they continued joking and jostling each other and heading directly for Ben without ever looking directly at him. It was easy to assume that they were just a raucous bunch of teenagers celebrating a successful competition. The thug with the gun held it down at his side to keep it out of sight. As the students passed between the two cars, bumping into Ben and the thugs, Ma stepped forward and, without looking, smashed the man with the gun on the temple with a back fist. The man fell unconscious to the pavement, dropping the gun which Ben kicked under the car. Ma's entourage quickly dispatched the other two. Ben never had a chance to hit one of them with his pole. If the thugs had guns, they didn't have a chance to get them out. It was over as quickly as it had started.

Ben checked to see that all three men were out of commission. Then he turned to the students.

"Thanks, guys, that was quick work. They never knew what hit them."

Ben faced Ma and gave a short bow, "I am in your debt, sir."

Ma bowed in return, "We offer Kung Fu with extended protection plan."

Ma's students erupted in laughter. In part as a relief to the tension of combat but also because most had never heard Master Ma make a joke before.

Detective Townsend appeared as if on queue. He was just finishing a call for backup on his police radio. Ben slid the gun out from underneath the car with his pole and Townsend picked it up with his pen and placed it in his handkerchief. He then went through the pockets of all three men finding two large switchblades.

"I followed them from the gym," said Townsend. "I figured that they might be after you."

"It appears that they were."

"Did they try to abduct you at gunpoint?"

"That they did."

"Good, that's a serious charge. If you come down to the station and make a statement to that effect, we'll have them where we want them."

Two police cars roared into the parking lot and three uniformed policemen, practically the entire police force, jumped out. The Frenchmen were cuffed and bundled into the cars in short order.

"Where do you want us to put them, sir? We're a little short of space." asked one of the officers.

Townsend responded, "Doesn't matter. Throw them in with the rest. They all work for the same organization. Oh, by the way, don't forget to let our FBI friends know. They'll want to be in on this, if not take credit for it."

Townsend walked back to Ma and his students, "That was a pretty courageous thing you did. And the acting. Good acting. You had everybody fooled. I thought you were a bunch of rowdy, drunken teenagers."

"We don't drink, sir," said one of the students.

Townsend shook his head, "No, I guess that you don't. Good job, Mister Ma. Later, I may ask you and some of your students to come down to the station to make some statements as witnesses."

"No problem," said Ma, "you know where to find us."

As Ma and his students left, Townsend pulled Ben aside.

"You've had quite a bit of excitement lately, Professor. We seem to be putting a lot of pressure on their organization."

"Yes, whoever they are, they seem to react quickly with more manpower."

"I think that the demise of this last bunch might slow them down for a while. Did you see her in the stands?"

"Her?" asked Ben.

"Come on. Marie, in the hooded sweatshirt. I saw you looking at her. You almost got your head knocked off looking at her. My, that Ma is something else."

"It might not have been her."

"Right, I was going to follow her until I spotted the three stooges watching you. If you have contact with her again please try to persuade her to come in."

"I will. You know I will."

"Well, I'll bet that these three came out of the same mold as the other two. At this point we've arrested five or six hoodlums, not sure about Taflon, from the same organization. That should make it a little difficult to cover up. We'll see what the FBI and the French police can make of that."

Ben drove home and parked in front of the garage. A dark form approached him from the shadows by the back door.

"Don't hit me with your stick, Ben. It's me, Marie."

Ben dropped his gear bag and pole and put his arms around her.

"I was afraid that they had seen you at the tournament."

"They only had eyes for you. But it was a bit too close so, after your act—"

"Demonstration."

"After your demonstration, I split, as you say. Did they come after you?"

"Yes, they tried but I had some help and all three are in the local jail."

"*Magnifique*. Some help you said?"

"Master Ma, the Chinese man I did the demonstration with, and his students. Your three compatriots tried to grab me in the parking lot. Ma and his students laid them out."

"Wish I could've seen it. By the way you were very impressive…"

"Thank you."

"…for an old man."

Ben held her tight, "Thanks a lot. And to think that I worried about you."

"Take me inside. I think that I can spend the night if you'll have me."

"I'll have you."

Morning

The next morning Ben awoke to the smell of coffee. Marie stood over him dressed in one of his undershirts holding two steaming mugs. The undershirt was of the wife-beater variety and much too large for her. She had trouble keeping it from slipping off her shoulders. She would look good in anything, thought Ben.

"Ah, to awake to the smell of coffee and the touch of a bare breast against one's cheek," he said.

"You had enough bare breast last night." She laughed. "You'll have to settle for coffee and conversation. Now tell me about that Venezuelan girl you were kissing at Peckham's."

"What? Who told you that?"

Marie laughed. "I have a friend I stay with when I'm not with you. She happened to be at the pub last Thursday night. She told me she was very impressed with your playing, especially the Villa-Lobos duet with a beautiful Venezuelan girl who kissed you. I was very jealous."

"She only kissed me on the top of the head," said Ben.

"I know. I'm just having fun. But I was very jealous that you were making wonderful music with someone else."

"I would love to make wonderful music with you."

"We will, we will."

The morning light provided Marie with her first good look at the wound above Ben's eye. She put the coffee mugs on the bedside table and went to the bathroom in search of first aid materials. She returned with everything she could find.

"Hold still, this bandage needs changing."

She peeled off the old band aid and cleaned the area around the cut. The butterfly that Ben had applied was doing well, so she left it intact.

"I noticed this last night when you were doing your demonstration. How did it happen?"

"Two of your countrymen were waiting for me when I got home the night before last."

"My countrymen?"

"Two thugs from Marseille."

"What..."

"They were waiting for me in my house and they just started beating on me. To make a long story short, I got ahold of my pole and dispatched them."

"Dispatched? Is that a Kung Fu term?"

"I guess it is. You know, hit them on the head, they fall down and don't get up right away."

"I understand," she said with a laugh as she touched his head near the wound again.

"Anyway they're in jail with Hakim and the other three from last night."

Marie applied Neosporin and a new band aid without comment. She then sat cross-legged on the bed next to Ben and sipped her coffee.

"I recognized one of the three men at the tournament," she said.

"From where?"

"From France. He was with Thérèse one night when she visited Paris and we got together for dinner. I don't think they were a couple, just traveling together. He dropped her off at our dinner rendezvous so I only talked with him for a few moments. I don't remember his name. I believe that he also worked for Bonsans, but I don't know for sure."

"Which one was he? Can you describe him?"

"The older, no oldest, one. That is correct, no?" she asked.

"What's correct?"

"Oldest."

"Yes, oldest of three, older of two."

"Thank you."

"Marie, the police need to know this."

"Then tell them."

"Why don't *you* tell them?"

"Sorry, Ben. They might lock me up just to protect me. Or, at least, they would have someone following me around. And I've got things to do."

"Well, you may not have much time. The FBI is now involved and will probably set up a task force. Sooner or later, they will stumble across you if the bad guys don't find you first."

"A task force for one murder?"

"They think that the murder had to do with a drug smuggling operation."

"Thérèse would never be involved with drug selling. Hakim maybe. Don't they know about the Gerard text?"

"Yes, of course, but they don't believe it."

"What part don't they believe?" she asked.

"They don't believe that there *is* a treasure and they don't believe that *she* was killed for the text."

"*Incroyable*," she said shaking her head.

"Well," said Ben. "They're the FBI. 'Often wrong but never in doubt,' according to Detective Townsend."

"Oh, I almost forgot," said Marie. "Could you go by my apartment and rescue my cello? The apartment is no longer taped off as a crime scene but I'm afraid that if I go back there I'll be recognized. And besides I can't be lugging a cello around for the next few days."

"Is there anything else you need?"

"No, I took the important things when I left. Well, most of them. A short black dress, perhaps."

"Can't become attached to material things," he said.

She punched him in the ribs. "You're terrible."

"What do you want me to do with the cello?"

"Just keep it here for me."

"That means I get to see you again?"

Marie took Ben's flippant comment very seriously. "Oh, Ben, do you ever think about how things would have been without this terrible mess?"

"I know that I would've done everything I could to convince you to be with me."

"And now?"

"And now, you're on a solo mission and I'm just supposed to wait for the outcome."

Marie didn't respond. She walked over to Ben's guitar sitting on a stand in the corner and brought it back to him.

"Play something for me," she said as she lay on the bed next to him.

Without comment Ben sat up in bed and played Riera's *Nostalgia*. It was a simple piece that just seemed to match their mood. When he finished Marie had tears in her eyes. He set the guitar on the floor next to the bedside table and wrapped his arms around her.

"I want you in my life," he said. "And I want to help you deal with this."

"Ben, please be patient with me. I know you think I'm weak because I cry with you always. I'm not a weak person. I know that you want to help, but just be patient a little longer. This terrible mess is almost over. And somehow, don't ask me how I know but, I know that we will be together again when it's done."

"I wish I had the same confidence," he said.

They lay on the bed in each other's arms until they fell asleep.

Ben's phone rang. He picked up the bedside extension and looked at Marie as he answered.

"Ben Slade."

"Good morning, Professor. Townsend here. Sorry to bother you so early, but the Feds…the FBI people want to talk to you first thing this morning. First thing for them is about nine o'clock."

"Talk about what, might I ask?"

"You might. Now that you've helped round up a significant sampling of the low life of Marseille, they are convinced, more than ever, that this whole thing has to do with a big drug ring. And they want to know how *you* are involved."

"Did you tell them that I'm just a simple math professor?"

"I wouldn't want to prejudice their investigation."

"Great. Thanks a lot."

"Ha. You know that they don't pay attention to anything that I say anyway. Come down to my office about ten to nine and I'll take you over to their new command center. I'll stick with you during the interrogation if you'd like."

"I'd like," said Ben as he hung up.

"I have to go talk to the FBI," he said to Marie.

"You won't tell them that I'm here, will you?"

"No, of course not. I don't like what you're doing but I won't try to stop you."

Marie leaned over and gave him a kiss.

"Do you need money?" he asked.

Marie laughed. "Thanks, I already took a little."

"What's a little?"

"Two hundred."

"Two...did you leave me anything?"

"Ten dollars...and sweet memories."

Marie kissed him again.

"Will you come back tonight? You might be safer here."

"Maybe, I'll see. Like don't be worried if I don't."

"*Like*, you've caught it," said Ben. "And you've only been in America a short time."

"Caught what?"

"The unfinished simile, *like*...the parasite of American English," he said.

"Unfinished like Schubert?"

"The same."

Marie laughed. "Very funny. It's very infectious, I agree. Like a bad weed. That *like* is okay, no?"

"No, yes, just fine," he said as he gave her a hug.

"Marie, I almost forgot. Have to know something. That first night, when I helped you solve the longitude problem, you made a quick phone call to someone in French. Who did you call?"

Marie sat up straight.

"Why do you want to know?" she asked.

"Detective Townsend thinks it's important, maybe key to the events leading to your sister's death."

Marie hung her head.

"Thérèse. I called Thérèse."

Interrogation

At 8:50 am Ben walked into Detective Townsend's office. Townsend was on the phone but he smiled and offered Ben a chair while he finished his conversation and hung up.

"Right on time," said Townsend. "Come on, I'll walk you over to the FBI team's new office."

"In the Excelsior?"

"Exactly. In the bridal suite. It appears that nobody's getting married in the next couple of weeks."

The Excelsior Hotel was an imposing stone structure built post Civil War to demonstrate the rising fortunes of the New England industrialists. It had always operated as a hotel and had always been well maintained, although its attached theatre had since been replaced by an almost modern office building. Townsend seemed amused at having the FBI in the bridal suite. The ballroom had been booked for the graduation formal and was probably too large anyway. The bridal suite was the next logical choice.

Before they reached the door of the suite, Ben paused and said, "I think that it's all right to talk to these guys without a lawyer, but if it appears to you at any point that I need some legal help, just cough twice."

"Will do."

Ben and Townsend knocked and entered. A large folding table had been set up in the middle of the room. The three FBI agents, all in dark grey suits, labored over papers on one side and a single empty chair had been placed on the other. Perfect for grilling by intimidation, thought Ben. The investigation was being run by Agent James Pike, III, a thirty-something man with a serious demeanor and a military hair cut. On his left was Agent Burrell who looked like he was cut from the same cloth as Pike. On Pike's right was Agent Driscoll, a slim attractive woman in her late twenties. Attractive despite the fact that she had done everything possible with her makeup and pulled-back hair to make her appearance severe and stern. What a shame, thought Ben.

Agent Pike nodded to Ben and pointed to the empty chair. He turned to Townsend, "You, of course, are welcome to stay, but it's not necessary."

Ben suppressed a smile. There was obviously bad blood between Pike and Townsend. Ben was pretty sure that Townsend hadn't hidden his disdain for the "federal suits."

"I fully intend to stay," said the detective as he pulled up a chair on the end of the table, symbolically in the neutral zone. Pike looked as if he were going to say something but thought better of it and returned his attention to Ben. Ben was still on his feet waiting for the exchange to finish. Agent Pike shot him a look that was supposed to wither.

Ben was unaffected. "Here?" he asked pointing to the lone chair. His eyes met Agent Driscoll's for a moment and she looked down struggling to suppress a smile. Thank god, thought Ben. *She's still in there.*

Agent Pike took control. "Mr. Slade—"

"Professor Slade," interrupted Townsend. "In this town, we call professors Professor."

Agent Pike gritted his teeth and continued, "Professor Slade, our discussion will be recorded. Is that okay with you?"

"Yes."

"It appears that you agree to talk to us without counsel. Is that correct?"

"Yes, I've agreed to talk to you to help with the investigation, but if the interrogation turns to suspected wrongdoing on my part, I will suspend the session until I can be legally represented."

"Fair enough," said Pike. "What kind of wrongdoing might you be suspected of?"

"You *are* investigating a murder, are you not?"

"Yes, of course," said Pike, "but we don't think that you're the murderer."

"Thanks for that."

"We have reason to believe that the murder victim or the intended murder victim was involved in an international drug ring which lead to her death."

"I see," said Ben frowning.

"We have six people in custody, all of whom have suspected links to drug trafficking in Europe."

"Not surprising. Five of them are thugs from Marseille."

Agent Pike seemed to be surprised.

"How do you know that?" he asked.

"It's a small town," said Ben, not wanting to implicate Townsend.

"Had you ever met any of the six before they were apprehended?'

"The five thugs, no. I had seen Hakim once before in Marie's apartment."

"The night of the murder."

"Yes."

"And days later, he tried to contact you?"

"No, he was scouting around my boat when Detective Townsend and I spotted him."

"Why would he do that?"

"I don't know."

"I understand that your house was ransacked during the night of the murder?"

"That's correct."

"And you, presumably, were not there."

"Correct, I was on my boat."

"All night?"

"Yes, I slept on my boat."

"Why did you sleep on your boat?"

"I just went down to the boat to read and relax. And I fell asleep. Woke up at morning light."

"Do you sleep on your boat often?"

"No, at least not when she's in home port."

"The people who ransacked your house. What were they looking for?"

"I don't know for sure, but I suspect that it was the Gerard text."

"The book of French baroque poetry leading to buried treasure?" said Pike with a laugh. "I've been in this business long enough to know a red herring when I see one, or smell one."

Agent Pike exchanged glances with the agents on either side. Detective Townsend looked bored.

"I understand that you disappeared for a few days after the murder. We wanted to talk to you and you were nowhere to be found."

"I didn't disappear. I just went for a sail."

"To where?"

"Maine."

"Weren't you told to stay in town?"

"No, just to stay in the area."

"And you consider Maine 'in the area'?"

"I was in contact with Detective Townsend who, by the way, was not happy with my little trip."

"Did you sail alone?"

Ouch, thought Ben. He now had to make a choice.

"Sailing alone upwind was the reason it took me so long to get back."

Ben avoided looking at Townsend. Townsend continued looking out of the window and said nothing.

"Two of the men we've detained broke into your house the night before last. Is that correct?" asked Agent Pike.

"Yes, they were waiting for me in my living room when I got home."

"What did they want?"

"I don't know."

"How can that be? What did they say?"

"They didn't say anything. They just started hitting me."

Townsend interrupted, "Excuse me but when I asked you that question, I believe that you stated that 'They said ouch'."

Agent Pike exploded, "Detective, please. Your cavalier attitude isn't helping this investigation."

"Either is your preconceived notion of what happened," Townsend responded. "The two men were obviously looking for the text and/or Marie LaFontaine. The professor, here, was their only lead. And if he weren't a martial artist, we would probably be investigating his murder as well."

Pike lowered his head and took a couple of deep breaths, probably a technique learned in an anger management course. The other two agents looked uncomfortable and said nothing.

"Detective Townsend, this is *my* interrogation, *my* investigation. If you don't stop disrupting the proceedings, I will have you removed."

"Understood," said Townsend settling back in his chair.

The tension was broken by a knock at the door of the bridal suite. Evidently political correctness hadn't completely pervaded the FBI as Agent Pike nodded to Driscoll who dutifully got up and went to open the door. Ben noticed that she walked with an elusive double jiggle on the outer edge of each cheek. Elusive because it seemed to Ben that the double jiggle only appeared in athletic women who might not be as fit as they once were. Townsend watched Ben watching Driscoll's ass. When their eyes met Townsend raised his head and rolled his eyes. Agent Driscoll opened the door and ushered in a room service cart with coffee and croissants.

When they were all settled with their coffee, Agent Pike returned his attention to Ben, "I understand that you subdued your attackers. Is that correct?"

"Yes, sir."

"Did you speak to them after they were subdued?"

"No."

"Why not? Didn't you want to know what they wanted? Or did you already know?"

"I didn't speak to them because they were unconscious."

"And you had never seen them before?"

"Never."

"Last night there were three men who approached you after the martial arts tournament. Is that correct?"

"Yes."

"What did they want?"

"They wanted me to get into their car."

"But why? What did they want?"

"I don't know."

"You must know something. Don't you think it strange that five men from Marseille are after you and you don't know why?"

"I think I know why but it appears that you're not accepting that answer," said Ben.

Townsend laughed out loud. Agent Pike took another few deep breaths.

"Had you ever seen those three men before?"

"Yes."

Interrogation

Pike shifted in his chair. The answer seemed to take him by surprise.

"Where, when?"

"Earlier last night. They were in the audience at the tournament."

"Out of hundreds of people, you noted three men whom you had never seen before? That's hard to believe."

"Not so hard. They looked like thugs. Master Ma spotted them too. That's why he gathered his students and rescued me."

"Agent Pike," said Townsend, "I noticed them too. They stood out like a sore thumb."

Pike hung his head and closed his eyes before continuing with Ben.

"And you had never seen the three men before last night?"

"That is correct."

"Do you know that all five men plus the Algerian are linked to drug trafficking?"

"Well you just mentioned that but it doesn't surprise me."

"Do you use illegal drugs?"

"Not currently."

Detective Townsend had a short coughing fit.

"What kind of drugs have you used?"

"Marijuana while in school." Ben was about to add, 'but I didn't inhale' and stopped himself at the last moment. Unfortunately, the thought brought on a smile that he couldn't completely suppress.

"What's so damn funny?" asked Agent Pike.

"Nothing, sir."

"You don't seem to realize the trouble you're in. You're in the middle of something big and the best you can do is 'I don't know' which you've now told me three times. If you think you're pleading the fifth to your benefit, it's only making you look worse."

"Sorry, it's just the image of Clinton saying, 'but I didn't inhale' made me smile."

Townsend erupted in laughter. The other two agents tried not to smile. Agent Pike had no difficulty being serious.

"Any other drugs?"

"Excuse me?"

"Have you used any other illegal drugs?"

"No." Ben decided to ignore his experimentation with LSD.

"Have you ever sold illegal drugs?"

Townsend continued to cough.

"No, I haven't," said Ben.

"Would you be willing to take a lie detector test?"

"As I said at the onset, if this discussion turns to my suspected wrongdoing, then we're done until I find a lawyer."

"Do you know the whereabouts of Marie LaFontaine?"

"No, I don't," said Ben as he rose to his feet. By this time Marie would have left his house. It wasn't much of a lie.

"Not so damn fast," said Pike. "It just might serve the interests of justice to lock you up right now."

"Excuse me, sir," said Detective Townsend, "but don't you think that might a bit awkward since we have only two cells and they're filled with the lowlifes who were trying to threaten the professor, here?"

Agent Pike had to think for a minute. "Okay, but don't leave town, not to Maine, not anywhere. Don't leave town. Get a lawyer. We'll talk again. Probably tomorrow."

Detective Townsend was at the door ahead of Ben. The interrogation was over.

Ben and Townsend didn't talk until they reached the street.

"I see that you've established a warm rapport with the Feds," said Ben.

Townsend laughed. "Well, I do my best."

"Thanks for your help," said Ben. "They were clumsy and rough."

"Indeed they were. And it seems that in today's FBI, it's still the young ladies who are sent to get coffee."

"Oh, some new information. Marie told me that she briefly met the oldest thug of the three last night. She met him in Paris when he was travelling with Thérèse and it appeared that they worked for the same company, Bonsans."

"Yes, we've pretty much established that connection although there is no official link as yet."

"By the way, when the longitude problem was solved, the phone call that Marie made was to Thérèse."

"Marie told you?"

"Yes, last night."

"Thank you," said Townsend placing his hand on Ben's shoulder. "Things are beginning to fall into place."

"How does that help?"

"Evidently Thérèse entered the country about a week before, bought a cell phone giving a bogus name and address, and made contact with her sister."

"Yes, but—"

"We've been tracing the movements of that phone and collecting a list of all people called from it. We just weren't sure who it belonged to. Now, it's all starting to make sense."

"What sense? What do you suspect?"

"Thérèse was in Boston, probably helping to arrange a business deal for that Bonsans company. Two hours after Marie called her, she started driving up from Boston. On the way she called Frieda Rawlings' cell phone."

"Oh my god. Unbelievable."

They walked back to the station in silence. At the door Townsend shook Ben's hand.

"Go home," said the detective. "I'll try to get these clowns off your back. If you see Marie again, try to persuade her to come in. She's in real danger."

Payback

Ben stopped by his house to make sure that Marie wasn't still there. She wasn't but she had left a note.

Dear Ben,
I want you in my life too.
Please be patient. We will
get through this and I promise
not to cry so much in the future.
            Love,
            M.
P.S.- Stay away from beautiful, talented Venezuelan girls.

He picked up some food, beer, and wine and headed down to the marina.

The marina took up almost half of the small harbor, the rest being allocated to the commercial fishing fleet, or what was left of it. The dilapidated trawlers, tied up to equally dilapidated docks, were witness to the decline of commercial fishing in the area. The recreational boats in the marina, however, spoke of vitality, prosperity, and a love of tradition. Ben's *Emma*, a classic cutter and lovely to look at, was just one of the many well-cared-for traditional craft in the harbor. The best examples dated back a hundred years to Herreshoff designs and it took a keen nautical eye to distinguish between those newly built boats based on Herreshoff's original designs and those boats that were actually a century old.

He had just boarded *Emma* when George Rawlings pulled up. George looked worse than before. His clothes appeared slept in but George didn't look like he had had much sleep.

"Called your house," said George. "Figured you'd be down here. Do you have a few minutes? I need to talk to someone."

"Anytime. Come aboard and I'll get you a beer."

They sat in the cockpit with their beers on a beautiful late spring day.

"What's up?" asked Ben.

"Do you remember that I told you that Frieda was in Zurich on business?"

Ben nodded.

"Well, she's not. I happened to see her credit card charges online. She's been in and around Besançon in France."

"What's wrong with that?"

"Besançon is the place where our François Gerard looted the chateau. Frieda has been over there trying to find the treasure."

"How would she know where to look?"

"She knows as much about it as I do. I shared Marie's findings with her because she thought that it was all so exciting."

"Still, would that be enough to know where to look?"

"I don't know, but she took a great interest in Bonsans, that company that Marie's sister worked for. And then that Algerian, who also works for Bonsans, shows up at the house asking for her."

"What are you getting at?" asked Ben.

"I think that Frieda has been involved in this whole damn thing from the beginning."

"That's hard to believe. Do you have any real proof?"

"No hard proof but too much points that way. Anyway when Frieda called this morning, I confronted her with what I thought."

"What did she say?"

"She just laughed. She admitted to 'having a bit of a look' for the treasure but she said that it was a wild goose chase. According to her, if the treasure still exists, it's buried beneath the parking lot of a shopping mall west of Besançon."

The issue of the longitude correction flashed through Ben's mind but he said nothing. The possibility of Frieda's involvement in Thérèse's murder took its place. It was impossible for him to picture Frieda as a murderer.

Ben said, "Yes, Frieda has or had some kind of relationship with Bonsans. The police have already established that, but do you really think that she had anything to do with the murder?"

George looked down and shook his head.

"I don't know. I really don't know. She's coming home tonight. Maybe I'll ask her."

The two friends sat without further discussion for a good half hour. Finally, George got up, thanked Ben for the beer, and drove home.

Ben continued to tinker around on the boat through most of the afternoon, fixing things that didn't really need to be fixed. His mind was awash with too many currents and there was nowhere else he would rather be. He was still smarting from the clumsy FBI interrogation. How could the FBI agents be so sure and so wrong? And now George suspects that Frieda has been mixed up in this from the beginning. Could she have been involved in the murder? Where was Marie and what was she up to? Sooner or later she would be caught, probably by the wrong people. She wasn't superwoman although, in many aspects, he had to admit that she was close.

"Ahoy, Captain, do you need any crew?"

Ben peered over *Emma's* rail into Skip's sunny face. His mother, Evie, bounced down the dock close behind. What a breath of fresh air. Ben's mental gyrations weren't producing anything positive anyway.

"Absolutely, Skip. Do you think that your mother would like to come too?"

"To tell you the truth, Captain, she was the one who suggested it."

"Skip, dear," protested Evie, "you don't need to tell everything you know."

"How are you, Evie?" asked Ben.

"Never better, but you look a little worse for wear. Walk into another door?"

"Something like that, but you should see the other guys."

"No need. The story is all over town. Makes you sound like King Kong with a stick. Enrollment at Master Ma's Kung Fu Studio is way up."

"Come aboard and I'll tell you what really happened. It was dark and all over in thirty seconds. Hardly the stuff of legends."

Ben revved up the old engine and had his crew cast off. On their way out of the harbor Evie asked, "Ben, why is it that those two big boats over there have red lights on the top of their masts at night, but the others, and yours, don't?"

"Right. In the States if your mast is over one hundred feet tall, you have to display a red light on the top, even at anchor."

"So the airplanes won't hit it," ventured Skip.

"Exactly," said Ben.

"But that one," said Evie, "doesn't look as high and I've noticed that it too has a red light at night."

"Well, some people like to light up for the prestige."

"Oh, like mast envy," said Evie.

Ben broke out in a laugh that he couldn't control.

"What's mast envy?" asked Skip.

Nobody answered. Finally Ben said, "Your mother will explain it later."

"Yeah, much later," said Evie.

Ben and his crew spent the rest of the afternoon sailing up and down the coast outside the harbor. Skip learned how to handle the helm to come about after he mastered the 'ready about, hard to lee' which, as he pointed out, made no sense in modern English. Evie tended the genoa sheets and preserved the moments with her new digital camera. Nobody cared that they didn't go very far.

Returning to the dock about six o'clock, they tied up *Emma*. As the crew departed Ben shook Skip's hand.

"Master Skip, you're becoming a real sailor."

"Thank you, Captain, anytime you need crew, just whistle."

Evie gave Ben a kiss on the cheek with a quiet 'thank you.'

Then she said to Skip, "Go back to the diner and get my purse from the changing room and then we'll head home."

"Okay, Mom," said Skip as he ran off.

Evie turned back to Ben, "I don't want you to take this the wrong way but I think that it's good for Skip to be with you. As they say, he needs a man in his life."

"What about his father?"

"Skip thinks his father is dead. Some time ago I thought that it was a better story than what really happened. Eventually, he'll have to know the truth. Anyway I want you to know that he loves to sail and he thinks you're great and I don't have to be part of the package. I'm just happy—"

"Wow," Ben said with a smile, "that's about as direct as it gets."

Evie turned and started walking down the dock.

"I'm reeling from something right now," said Ben.

"Yes, I know you are," she said as she kept walking.

"But I think that it's a great package," he called after her.
Evie didn't turn back but put a little hop in her step.

Ben went home to an empty house. He took two steaks out of the freezer with the hope that Marie would come back. He took a nap. And then he woke up and tried some chess problems but they weren't holding his interest. He practiced guitar for an hour. Finally he grilled one of the steaks and put the other back in the fridge. Some frozen butternut squash ravioli, boiled on the stove, completed the meal. Ben wasn't a worrier, but he was definitely worrying. At their last meeting, Marie had not been quite her buoyant self. Preoccupied and even somewhat depressed. And her statement that 'this mess is almost over' kept breaching his thoughts. What did she mean? What was she planning? It was a long, bad night. He almost finished the bottle of Château du Pez he had opened for dinner before he fell into an empty bed.

At four in the morning, Detective Townsend woke Ben by banging on the front door. Ben put on a bath robe and let him in. On his way to the front door Ben noticed someone with a flashlight outside the back door. Townsend was all business.
"Is she here?"
"Who?" Ben was having trouble waking up.
"Marie, of course."
"No, I haven't seen her since yesterday morning."
"Do you know where she is?"
"No, she never tells me where she goes."
Townsend opened the back door and told the policeman there that he could return to the police station.
"Sit down," said Townsend, "the shit has hit the fan."

Ben splashed some water on his face and sat opposite the detective at the kitchen table.

"Frieda Rawlings was murdered last night on her way home from the airport," said Townsend.

"Frieda. I can't believe it."

"We think that Marie had a hand in it."

"Why would you think that? I don't think that she's—"

"Let me tell you what happened and *you* be the judge. Mrs. Rawlings preferred to use the limo service to and from Logan when she traveled abroad instead of making a local flight connection. Expensive, but I guess that she can afford it. Or could. Last night, the limo driver was getting a cup of coffee while waiting for her flight. He claims that he was distracted by a conversation with a beautiful woman while his limo was stolen. Mrs. Rawlings was picked up as usual and found dead in the limo about twenty miles north of the airport."

"My god."

"It almost looked like a professional hit with one in the forehead, small caliber fired from the front seat, and one in the heart."

"You said, 'almost'," iterated Ben.

"The wound to the heart was caused by a knife, which was still in her chest."

Ben felt the wound. Not for Frieda, but for Marie. *Why couldn't she have allowed the system to work?*

Townsend continued, "I know that she's been in and out of here all week. That's been okay. But now she's wanted as a murder suspect and if you harbor her, you'll end up in jail."

"I understand."

"I know that you've become close to Marie and, if it makes you feel any better, I can tell you that Frieda Rawlings, in all likelihood, was responsible for Thérèse's death."

"George Rawlings told me yesterday that he discovered that Frieda had been in France looking for the treasure," said Ben.

"There was some kind of deal going on between Frieda and Thérèse or between Frieda and that French company that Thérèse worked for," said Townsend.

"Bonsans."

"Right. We still don't know exactly what was going on and we may never know since the two principals are both dead. However, it appears that Marie was going to be left out in the cold. My guess is that Thérèse found out or changed her mind and the two sisters tried to keep the treasure for themselves. Thérèse and Frieda had it out in Marie's apartment and Thérèse ended up dead."

"Apart from the phone records, is there any proof?"

"Let you know later in the day. We have DNA from under Thérèse's fingernails. There were signs of a struggle if you remember. If Frieda's DNA provides a match then that murder is as good as solved."

"And you think that you've solved Frieda's murder as well?"

Detective Townsend paused, "They shouldn't have used a knife in the chest."

"*They?*" asked Ben.

"The second limo driver, the one who stole the limo and picked up Frieda, was an elderly gentleman in uniform no less. We have a security camera video from the pickup area at the airport."

"And the beautiful woman?"

"Nothing on camera but a good description. Tall, long blond hair, probably a wig, dark glasses, very classy looking woman."

"Could have been anyone," said Ben.

"Of course, but do you really think that it *wasn't* Marie?"

Resolution

Ben went back to bed but sleep wasn't a remote possibility. Yes, he was sure that the woman decoy involved in Frieda's murder was Marie. No, he had no idea who the elderly gentleman second chauffer was. And he was reasonably sure that Marie had fled and that he would never see her again. He made a mental note to contact George later in the day to see if there was anything he could do for him.

Ben made some coffee about eight o'clock and started doing some Kung Fu exercises. Similar to Tai Chi but perhaps a harder, more physical form. Always good to clear the mind, although today they didn't seem to have much effect. His orderly life, so disrupted in the past two weeks, was back and laid out before him. And it looked boring. The excitement, the torment, the intrigue, all gone as abruptly as they had entered his life. And the wonderful Marie, gone. In the corner next to his guitar sat her cello, the only evidence he possessed that she had actually existed.

Townsend called him about eleven o'clock.

"Some news, Professor."

"Thanks for phoning."

"We have a match of DNA. Frieda and Thérèse were definitely going at it when Thérèse was killed."

"Last week I would have sworn that it wasn't possible."

"And Boston police have picked up the second limo driver. He was only making a half-hearted attempt to escape. You might be able to guess his name."

"What? I've no idea. Wait…"

"That's right. Jean LaFontaine, the father of Marie and Thérèse."

"Oh, my god."

"On the way to the police station, he collapsed so they took him to Mass General. Turns out that he's in the final stages of cancer."

"Was he the shooter?"

"Proudly admits to everything and, yes, he had fired a gun last night. Claims that the beautiful blond decoy was just a fortuitous coincidence."

"Do you believe that?" asked Ben.

"Of course not."

"Are you going to pursue her?"

The detective paused, "We showed a picture of Marie, and others, to the real limo driver. He couldn't be sure if she was the lady who distracted him. Seems like the makeup and the blond wig had him confused. Not to mention the cleavage."

"The cleavage?"

"Yes, when pressed, the driver admitted that the lady wore a very low cut dress and that he spent more time looking at her breasts than her face."

"Perhaps he could make a positive identification of her breasts," said Ben with a laugh.

"Indeed. So with regard to Marie, we have motive, big time, but nothing else and you need more than motive to prosecute. I'd like to talk to her, but I'm not starting a search for her if that's what you mean."

"Thanks. Don't take me wrong but I'm a bit surprised."

"Because?"

"Because I would have thought that you would want justice done to the letter of the law."

"Justice *was* done, just not to the letter as you say. In my way of thinking, the big problem with taking the law into your own hands is that your emotions are in control and you might make a mistake and kill the wrong person. In this case they got it right."

"Glad for that," said Ben.

"The judicial system would have eventually arrived at the same result, perhaps with a life sentence instead of a death sentence. But consider the other side of the issue. Say the judicial system screws up, for example, because of shoddy police work or some lawyer's mistake and a known killer gets to walk. That's just as bad, maybe worse. In that case if somebody, on their own, were to remove the killer from society, I might be inclined to look the other way."

"Because justice was done."

"Exactly. In Marie's case there is not one shred of evidence in the limo or on the knife or gun to link her to Frieda's execution. We don't even have a reliable eye witness placing her at the airport. So even if I were determined to go after her, it would be futile."

"I understand," said Ben.

"But there's the matter of the FBI. It's difficult to weave two knives in the chest and old Jean LaFontaine, who was a retired, respected physician in Bandol, into this international drug ring theory of theirs."

Ben chuckled. "Well, with their alternative logic, I'm sure that they could come up with something."

"Possibly. The point is that I don't know what they'll do. They may declare that the murders are solved and take their six drug-related detainees back to Boston to make a case against them. Or they may decide that Marie is the ring leader and take off after her."

"I hope not."

"In any case, with all the confusion of the second murder, I think that they've dropped you as prime suspect and possible drug lord."

"That's just fine with me."

"Well, Professor, that leaves us with just one item of unfinished business."

"What's that?"

"Our chess game."

Two days later, the FBI team declared victory and returned to Boston with their drug ring. A large paddy wagon roared into town to empty out the local jail causing some stir in the small community. Townsend simply noted that the bridal suite was again available in case anybody wanted to get married.

It took Ben two days to get his emotions under control and start thinking rationally again. Upon resurfacing, he phoned the Rawlings house but received no answer, not even an answering machine. Next he tried George's office and reached the department secretary, Alice.

"Hello, this is Ben Slade. I'm trying to find George."

"Oh Professor Slade, I'm so glad you phoned. We're terribly concerned about Professor Rawlings. He came in yesterday, packed up most of his things, and left without speaking to a soul."

"I see," said Ben.

"I've tried several times to call him at home but never got an answer. I know that you two are good friends and I think he needs one now. Would you mind stopping by his house?"

"Of course, if I couldn't reach him, that was what I was going to do."

"And please, if you will, let me know how he is and if there is anything we can do."

"I will, Alice. Thank you for your concern."

Ben drove to the Rawlings' house and let himself in by the back door when no one answered. He found George in his study slumped over his desk. Ben's first impression was that George was dead but the sounds of labored breathing let him know that George had only passed out. Empty vodka bottles littered the bar. Ben went to the kitchen, made some coffee, and returned with a mug to an awakened George.

"What's that you've got?" asked George.

"Medicine for what ails you."

"It smells awfully strong."

"You look like you need something awfully strong. Here, start on this."

Ben returned to the kitchen to pour himself a mug. When he came back George was, at least, sitting up straight in his desk chair looking out the window.

"I'll never understand it," said George. "I can understand the excitement of locating the treasure, but killing someone for it is beyond comprehension."

"We'll never completely know what happened."

"Well, it was driven by greed, that much seems to be clear. And that's the part I can't fathom."

"Why?"

"Frieda was a trust fund baby with more money than we could spend if we tried. It just doesn't make sense."

"Maybe having more is important, not how much you have."

"Must be. But I thought that we were happy as we were. It appears that she wasn't. Have you heard from Marie?"

"Not a word. I'm sure that she's left the country. It's possible that I'll never see her again."

"So she got to you, did she?"

"I have to admit that she did. I've only known her for a couple of weeks but she left a big hole when she disappeared. I never realized that my life was so boring before her."

"Do you think she had a hand in Frieda's death?" asked George.

Ben paused. "Yes, I'm afraid that I do."

"Are the police going after her?"

"I'm not sure but I don't think so."

"I hope not," said George. "It's best left the way it is."

"Thanks. I'm glad you see it that way. Look, I passed a realtor's sign in your front yard. Are you moving?"

"Yes, I can't stay here after all this. The bedroom, the kitchen, every bush we planted together, every tree—they all smack me in the face. I've resigned my position at the university. I'm going to find something else, somewhere else."

"Jesus, Gorge, don't you want to give it a little more time?"

"Time will heal all?"

"Time for feelings to calm down. Time to forget. You're respected here. You've got friends here."

"Thanks for that, but no, I don't think I'm strong enough to wait for time to deal with things. I'll get settled somewhere and let you know where I am. We'll get together to play squash and go fly fishing."

The two friends sat with their thoughts for a minute or two.

"Make sure that you do," said Ben as he got up. George feebly arose from his chair and the two friends gave each other a long hug. Ben left with tears in his eyes.

Ben was also starting to look like a major casualty. With Marie gone, the ghost, or at least the memory, of Christine came back to haunt him. Her passive critique of him had been: "Why would an intelligent, vital person throw away their life in the cold middle of nowhere researching topics that probably wouldn't be useful for a hundred years, if even then?" He had laughed at the argument back then, noting that Laplace and Lagrange had done ground-breaking work that was only found really useful a century or more later. Perhaps his work would be the same. It was true that only a handful of people had read his dissertation. Perhaps a hundred had read his published papers. True, but not many people were interested in such an abstract, esoteric field as his. But someday it would be recognized and venerated, like the greats of mathematics. If only he really believed it. Christine's view of him and his life was becoming overpowering.

The coming fall semester contained a looming milestone for Ben. Early in his academic career he had befriended Professor Mike McCann whom he considered to be one of the best teachers he had ever known. One evening over a pint in a pub, McCann had revealed, "When you teach a course the first time it's challenging since you have to gather the material. The second time you teach the same course it's rewarding since you can tweak the contents and add your philosophy as to where the course material fits in the grand scheme of things. The third time you teach that course it's boring and every time after that, torture."

McCann's confession had made an indelible impression on Ben. At first he hadn't believed it was true but he had never forgotten it. Now he had taught the undergraduate Symbolic Logic course three times. McCann's judgment was 'spot on' as he would have said. Ben had gone through challenging, rewarding, and boring. The math department couldn't seem to find another professor to handle the course and Ben was looking at a semester of torture.

He started thinking seriously about taking a year off and sailing *Emma* to the Caribbean. He hadn't been at his current position long enough to merit a sabbatical, but maybe something could be worked out short of resigning. He bought cruising guides of the Windward and Leeward Islands and studied them in the evenings. Navigational charts and seasonal weather charts soon followed. Ben realized that he was indulging in pipe dreams like half of the middle-aged sailing population but it didn't matter. He needed a break, a change of life, and sailing was the only thing that stirred his interest.

Ben and Townsend had their chess game. In fact they settled into a routine of playing once a week, the loser from the previous week providing the pizza. Townsend was one of those players who can think ahead three, four, maybe five moves. This gave him a brilliant end game that more than made up for his ignorance of standard openings. Unless Ben was a piece or two pawns ahead when they got to the end game, Ben was almost sure to lose.

About mid-July while they were setting up the pieces for one of their matches, Ben asked, "Are you still working on the case?"

"No, it's been closed. We don't know everything but it's doubtful that we'll uncover anything new."

"But what about the details?"

"Like what?"

"Like who hired the guys in the cigarette boat?" asked Ben.

"That was Frieda. She knew where your first stop might be."

"But she didn't seem interested in the text."

"She wasn't. She already had a copy of the important pages. We found it in her luggage after she was killed."

"Then—"

"She was after Marie. She knew that Marie was still alive and would soon figure out who had killed her sister. Frieda knew that you had a relationship with Marie. She guessed correctly that Marie had fled with you."

"It seems that I was the last to know."

"By the way, we found the two guys who chased you. They were longshoremen from Portland. Both with long jackets. They borrowed a cigarette boat for the job, but had trouble returning it in the condition it was in after the collision with the trawler. We didn't have enough on them to make a case. It's not illegal to zoom around in the fog in Maine, just stupid."

"And what about the ransacking? Who did that?"

"It was our Algerian friend. Both places. That's something that we know pretty much for sure. He finally got talkative and I think that he was telling us the truth. He had been in Boston, probably setting up drug deals, when he was asked to contact George Rawlings, which he did, just as Marie told you. Then, when things started falling apart, he was instructed to obtain the text. He returned to Marie's apartment, found the body, and panicked. When he couldn't find the text in her apartment, he remembered you and assumed, rightly, that you had it. He found out where you lived and ransacked your place. And to answer your next question, the Bonsans people finally got nervous and sent over some muscle. Twice."

"So, any idea how Frieda ended up at Marie's apartment with Thérèse?"

"We know that Thérèse called Frieda on her way up from Boston. We're pretty sure that Frieda had a deal with Bonsans to share the treasure once Marie figured out where it was hidden. Thérèse must have arrived just after you left which must have been around midnight even though you tried to convince me otherwise."

"Yes, sorry about that."

"It's alright. I knew something was wrong but I never guessed that you were trying to cover up the fact that you had slept with her."

"Yes, that was hard to believe. Still is."

"It's not one hundred percent certain but we know that Marie and Thérèse spent some time together, probably planning how to keep the treasure for themselves. Then Marie left for some reason and Frieda arrived. Frieda sensed that she was being cut out of the deal and had a fight with Thérèse, killing her."

"Greed."

"Greed, indeed. Frieda already had copies of the important pages and enough information to find the treasure except for one little item."

"The longitude correction."

"Exactly. Thérèse probably knew about the correction but now she was dead. Frieda didn't know that a correction was necessary until she drew a blank in Europe. She probably thought that the whole thing was a hoax, which it might well have been. In any case Frieda left, Marie came home and found the body."

"Yes, she told me, as Thérèse, that she initially believed that the killers thought that they had killed Marie."

"Right, so she coolly made herself look more like her sister and hid out on your boat, not knowing that you were taking off for Maine."

Ben paused, "Well, I guess that just about wraps it up"

"Yes, as I said, there are a few details that we're not certain about, but it's unlikely that we'll learn anything new at this point."

"I'd have to agree."

"There is," said Townsend, "one other issue I'd like to raise with you."

"What's that?"

Townsend repositioned himself in his chair, "It's about Evie."

"Evie at the diner?"

"The same. You know, with all the publicity following the dual homicide we had here, there was a lot of interest in police work and forensics and things like that."

"Yes?" asked Ben wondering where all of this was going.

"Well, Evie's Skip, your sailing companion, along with two of his friends convinced their teacher to let them take on a forensic science school project before the end of the school year. We at the police station, well, I, helped them on their project. It turns out that Skip has a first class mind and is a hard worker to boot. A great kid. His chess game is still a bit sloppy but we're working on that. Well, one thing led to another and Evie and I got to know each other a little better."

"That's interesting," said Ben with a laugh. "I seem to remember her pushing your buttons pretty effectively that morning when I came back from Maine."

Townsend smiled. "Yes, she's bright and feisty. And she certainly knows how to push my buttons as you say."

"But why is this an issue that you would like to bring up with me?"

"Well, I know that you've taken them sailing and have had some kind of relationship with her and since you and I have…" Townsend paused.

"We've become friends, Richard. We're friends. Good friends, I'd like to think."

"Absolutely. Good friends. Anyway I'm interested in seeing if she would consider me as a…partner of sorts and I wouldn't want you to think that I was horning in."

Ben was quiet for a moment. "Look, I like Evie and I think she likes me, but her interest in me has always been as more as a father figure for Skip since he was interested in sailing and I was willing to take him out."

"Then you don't mind."

"I'm delighted. Sounds like you already have a good relationship with Skip which is probably essential in order to make any inroads with Evie."

"Already figured that one out," said Townsend with a smile.

As the summer dragged on, Ben tried to get back into his normal routine. He started developing some lectures for a special topics graduate course for the fall term but he couldn't get his head into it.

He read, worked out, and sailed. He missed Marie.

Late one afternoon in August, Ben and Townsend had settled into chess and pizza on the front porch of Ben's house. A FedEx delivery truck pulled up and the driver handed Ben a package.

"From Mustique," said the driver, "you must have friends in high places."

After the driver left, Ben was still holding the package, staring at the address label.

"Where's Mustique?" asked Townsend.

"It's a private island in the Grenadines. The rich and famous, like Mick Jagger and Princess Margaret, have had villas there."

"Aren't you going to open it?"

"I'll open it later."

"Open it now."

The package contained a first class plane ticket to Bequia, the nearest island to Mustique, and a note.

Dear Ben,
I owe you $810 and am now
in a position to repay you.
Please use this ticket. I will

send someone to pick you up
at the airport and bring you
back to the villa by boat.
I miss you.
>*Love,*
>*M.*

P.S.- I bought a cello and a guitar, a Ramirez.
>*Now we can make music together.*

Ben read the note in silence and then passed it to Townsend. Townsend read it and gave a long, low whistle.

"She found it, Ben."

"So it appears."

"And she wants to be with you."

"That's the hard part to believe."

Townsend picked up the ticket. "This is for a flight tomorrow."

"Do you think I should go?"

"Do you mean go to the woman who placed you in mortal danger, used you as a sex object, and repeatedly stole your money?"

"Well…"

"If you don't go, you'll be the biggest fool I've ever known."

The End

Acknowledgements and Notes

Author photo by Stephanie Halstead.

A multiple choice exam for a mathematical topic was actually used by Professor Leon Lasdon, currently at the University of Texas at Austin, with similar riotous results as those described in this book.

The author would like to acknowledge that the term 'mast envy' spoken by Evie in the Payback chapter originated with Harlan Crowder as witnessed by the author on St. Martin in 2004. Harlan is also the originator of the term 'user friendly' from his days at IBM.

Ben's Brazilian guitar teacher, Celso Machado is a renown classical guitarist and teacher although he lives, not in New England, but on the Sunshine Coast of British Columbia.

Mike McCann is a real person as well. He remains one of the best teachers I've ever known and he once told me the observation on teaching quoted here. I hope I've quoted it correctly.

Coach Copeland was a real track coach in Shelby, Ohio. The quotations here are his as well as I can remember them.

Master Ma is patterned after Feeman Ong, founder of a Kung Fu school in Akron, Ohio.

Friedrich Hameister flew Messerschmitt ME-109s for the Germans during WWII. He did not, as far as I know, make contributions to number theory.

Thanks to Pina Belperio of Whistler, British Columbia, for her help in preparing an early version of the manuscript.

Many thanks to Catherine Knepper of Iowa Wordwrights for her help in preparing the manuscript.

Finally, thanks to Stephanie Halstead for her untiring constructive criticism and inspiration.

About the Author

Tom Baker is a mathematician and a sailor. He was educated at ITESM in Monterrey, Mexico, Case Institute in Cleveland, Ohio, and Imperial College in London, England. He holds a Ph.D. in Systems Engineering. Tom's professional activities have been in the field of Operations Research. He has ten publications in professional journals including *Operations Research* and *Management Science*. For several years he served as an Associate Editor of *Operations Research*. After many years practicing Operations Research in industry and serving as the Coordinator of Operations Research for Exxon Corporation, Tom founded and directed a successful software and consulting company in the Supply Chain area. Along the way, he has managed to log over 54,000 miles in his own sailboats. He lives with his wife Stephanie and daughter Josephine on Vashon Island in Washington State.

T.E. Baker is the author of another Ben Slade novel—*A Sea Story*.

Made in the USA
Charleston, SC
11 January 2012